"Well, dinner is almost ready," my mother said, walking into the room. She looked at me and smiled. Then she turned to Caroline and Peter. "So, you two, when are you going to end the suspense and tell us what you named my granddaughter?"

Caroline grinned. "Peter and I decided that in honor of her uncle and *godfather*, Elliot . . . "

Elliot? Me?

" . . . we're naming her Elyse. Little Ellie."

"Little Ellie. How wonderful," my mother and father said almost at the same time. "Elliot, isn't that nice?" my mother asked.

"Nice," I said, sort of nodding, although I wasn't sure if having a girl named after you was nice or not.

"So, tell us, Elliot. How does it feel to be an uncle and a godfather?" Dad asked. "Elliot? . . . How does it feel?"

I lifted the baby from my lap.

"Wet."

The Wonder Worm Wars
Margie Palatini

HYPERION PAPERBACKS FOR CHILDREN

New York

For Mom, Auntie Anna, and Bob—M.P.

First paperback edition 1999.
Copyright © 1997 by Margie Palatini.
All rights reserved. No part of this book may be reproduced or
transmitted in any form or by any means, electronic or mechanical,
including photocopying, recording, or by any information storage
and retrieval system, without written permission from the publisher.
For information address Hyperion Paperbacks for Children,
114 Fifth Avenue, New York, New York 10011-5690.

Printed in the United States.
1 3 5 7 9 10 8 6 4 2
This book is set in 14.5-point Adobe Garamond.
Library of Congress Cataloging-in-Publication data
Palatini, Margie
The Wonder Worm Wars / Margie Palatini
cm.
Summary: Having a broken arm does not help nine-year-old Elliot com-
pete for attention with his young nephew and the overachieving girl who
has moved in next door to Elliot's best friend.
ISBN 0-7868-1352-0
[1. Family life-Fiction. 2.Babies-Fiction. 3. Jealousy-Fiction.]
Title.
PZ7.P1755Wo1997
[Fic]-dc21 96-50920

CONTENTS

WORD WAR ONE

"POND SCUM!"

"I'm going to get you for that, Elliot."

"Oh sure, Jonathan. A little toe cheese like you is going to get *me*."

"Will, too."

"Will not."

"Will, too."

"Will not."

Word war with a four-year-old. . . . Yeah. I'm a stinker.

"Take it back, Elliot."

"Make me, buffalo-breath boy."

The little guy took a wild swing at me. I ducked. What a move! Go to the videotape! I Michael Jordaned him around the living-room couch. Turn. Fake. Turn. Another amazing pivot past the end table by the El-Man. Then a hurdle over the old ottoman and one of those great grins that had taken every one of my nine and a half years to perfect.

Jonathan puffed like a blowfish. "You wait, Elliot."

"I'm wait-ing."

Jonathan scrunched his face, puckered his lips, and made one of those determined looks. "I'm . . . I'm . . . I'm going to . . . to . . . Oooh. I'm just going to smash you, Elliot!"

Determined. Yes, *very* determined.

"Ah-ah-ah. That's not nice," I said, wagging a finger. "And a little more respect there, if you don't mind. That's, 'I'm going to smash you, *Uncle* Elliot.' "

That really got him. Stopped him cold. He didn't know whether to scrunch, pucker, or actually say uncle.

Not that Jonathan ever called me "Uncle" Elliot. Not that I wanted him to, either. Hey—no way! When he first learned to talk, he barely got out "Elliot." What he actually got out was "Eweeit." Let me tell you, when someone calls you "Eweeit," you don't care what's in front of it. Especially the U word.

That's too weird, even for me. And I like weird.

But when your older sister makes you something as goofy as an uncle—without even asking your permission—well, that means war. It's your job—no, your duty, that's right, your duty—to be a worm to the squirt. And *I*, if I do say so myself, do my duty as the all-time incredible Wonder Worm himself. Don't get me wrong. Hearing Jonathan say uncle still gives me the shivers all right, but it's kind of worth it. . . . In a wormy sort of way.

We did a few more laps around the couch. Too easy. Too, too easy. I wasn't even breaking a sweat. Not a drip. Not a drop. I was beginning to think that maybe I was getting too old for this. Maybe the challenge of making his baby brain spin was gone. Maybe I should show him some mercy. . . . Maybe I should actually be nice. . . .

Naaaah.

Jonathan stopped running. He wiped his nose on his sleeve. "I'm going to tell."

Oh, brother. What a twerpido. "Tell who?" I asked. "Your mommy?"

As if I was afraid of my sister Caroline. I'm not

afraid of any sister who doesn't live under the same roof as I do. Those are the ones you really have to watch out for. And I still have two of those to worry about, so I don't get too scared of Caroline. It's Grace and Peggy who pinch.

Jonathan kept puffing. His lower lip was this close to a quiver. The tears were ready to drop. Plop. Plop. Plop. It looked like it was just about time for my good old, tried and true, word-war knockout puncheroo. I'd have him blubbering in a matter of seconds.

I was good, all right. I was really good. I was better than really good. I was a worm.

And in this corner, weighing in at a trim, all-muscle seventy-six pounds, the one, the only, Wonder Worm and still champion . . . EL-LIOT AL-CORN! (Crowd cheers—'Go, Worm, go!') And in this corner . . .

I looked at Jonathan. He looked at me.

Time out. Time out. His lip was not quivering. He wasn't even blinking back a tear. There he was, just leaning against the arm of the sofa, folding his arms in front of his chest with an I-know-something-you-don't-know look on his face.

I couldn't be losing my touch. . . . Could I?

"Then," he said.

"Then what?" I said right back with a so-what, in-your-face, name-your-game attitude.

"Then—I'm going to tell Grammie and Pop Pop on you."

Uh-oh. Game called on account of grandparents. They were Grammie and Pop Pop to him, but Mom and Dad to me. Jonathan was playing dirty now. He was out for blood. My blood!

"All right. All right," I said, staying calm. Playing it cool. Watching him watch me.

"All right what, Elliot?"

Wow. The little guy had guts. I was almost impressed. (Okay, I was impressed.) No problem. No problem. This just meant it was time for a little bit of the old Wonder Worm psychology. Jonathan was only four, he didn't know anything about that yet. I only figured it out myself last year when I was eight.

"All right," I said. "Go ahead. Tell them."

I held my breath. If this didn't work, I was guaranteed dead meat. Trust me. Parents act like different people when they become grammies and pop pops. It's like *The Invasion of the Body Snatchers*. They look like my parents. They sound like my parents. But they don't act like my parents. They are Jonathan's *grandparents*. Or grand-pod-parents. That means when I blow milk bubbles out of my nose, they say it's disgusting. When Jonathan does it, they run for the video camera.

They think Jonathan is the Albert Einstein of milk bubbles and sofa somersaults. Believe me, seeing your own mother and father turn into mushy grandparents right before your eyes is not a pretty sight. Body-snatched. There is no other logical explanation.

"I'm going to tell Grammie and Pop Pop."

He was confident, I had to give him that. But . . . I had psychology.

I looked him right in the eye. "No, you won't."

"Will, too."

So much for psychology. Jonathan didn't even blink. He knows his grammie and pop pop all right. Unfortunately, I knew them, too. I was starting to smell like dead meat. I went for broke.

"Won't," I said.

"Will, too," Jonathan said again.

"Won't."

"Will."

"Won't."

"Will."

Yes! Baited and hooked. Jonathan was such a sucker for word war. All thoughts of telling Grammie and Pop Pop went right out of his little head. The Wonder Worm squirms free again! I laughed. I think it was my last chuckle that put him over the edge. His nostrils flared and his face almost got as red as his T-shirt. Then his eyeballs got all bulgy. Something like blue marbles. He would have tackled me right there on the living room rug for sure except for one of my great turn-and-pivots past the coffee table—and—YES—I was out of there and running down the hall.

The sound of his Nikes pounded behind me, but my many years of getaway experience from three older sisters and a brother had him by a mile. I was a lean, mean, running machine, zigzagging through the kitchen, pushing open the back door, running out onto the deck and doing my famous Air Alcorn so-long-sucker crouch, leap, and jump over the railing and—

"Whoa! . . . Whoa! . . . WHOOOOA!"

2

THE GOOG

"DOES IT STILL HURT?"

Good old Goog. I could always count on him. The Goog and I were pals. Best friends since forever. His name wasn't really Goog, of course. It was Phillip. Phillip Gugliocello. But nobody called him anything but the Goog. Except maybe his grandmother.

"Nah," I said, rubbing the cast on my broken arm. "But everything inside is starting to itch. It feels like a million scillion ants are walking around in there."

"Cool," said Goog.

I nodded. "But itchy."

We leaned over the deck railing and stared at the squashed petunias. Or what was left of them. Now they just looked like one big mess of pink and purple mush. And those beans my mother was growing? History.

"So, that's where you landed, huh?" Goog asked.

"Crunch City," I said.

We tilted our heads to the right. From that angle you could almost make out the shape of my body in the smashed flowers. Legs. Feet. Butt. One little bean was still hanging on, just about where my arm twisted into a pretzel.

"What did your mom say?"

"Actually at first she was pretty teary. She even rubbed my hair and called me Sweetie."

"That was good," said Goog.

"That was great. I thought I was home free. The last time she did that was when I had the flu and I did a barf-o-rama all over her bed." I sighed. "But then . . ."

"Yeah? . . ."

"Then Jonathan had to go and tell her what I just told you. You know. Pond scum. Buffalo-breath boy. Word war. The works."

"Ooops. That's bad."

"The worst."

"Then what did she say?"

"Let me put it this way . . . I'm still taking out the garbage."

"Uh-oh."

"Tell me about it."

I thought having a broken arm would have at least some advantages. First dibs on the TV clicker. No baths. Everyone having to be nice to me. Especially my sisters. Even the doctor who patched me up in the emergency room at the hospital said I needed TLC. And I would have gotten it, too, if—if—if Jonathan hadn't blurted out his Squirt Bulletin. That tidbit of info zombified mom before I had a chance to come up with a good wormy explanation for my arm, the deck, her flowers, and of course being a stinker to the Squirt.

"Get this, Goog—my mom actually said, 'It's only a broken arm,' and I'll 'live.'"

"Cold."

"Very cold. Yesterday she even wrote out a new list of chores that I can do with one hand."

"Ouch."

"And, she made me take a bath . . . with a Baggie wrapped around my arm! Let me tell you something,

Goog—Billy Zakian is wrong. All wrong."

"Huh? What does Billy have to do with it?"

Goog didn't remember last year in Mrs. Fiore's class when Billy told everybody the Zakian Theory. I explained to Goog that Billy said the youngest kid in the family has it made. Guaranteed. He said when you're the firstborn kid you get stuck with early bedtimes, clean clothes, spinach, cauliflower. If you're born second, you don't have to eat so many vegetables and your parents don't get all crazy if you're not in bed before the sun sets. *But,* if you're born any number after that, or better yet, last—then your mom and dad are so tired from the kids that came before you, that pretty much everything is negotiable. Best of all, you never get yelled at or blamed for *anything*—even if you did it—because you're the baby in the family.

"That, according to Billy, is having it made," I said. "Billy Zakian is the youngest kid in his family. He has it made. *I'm* the youngest kid in my family. . . . Do I have it made? Uh-uh. I have Jonathan. Billy didn't figure in the Jonathan factor."

"Oooooh."

"Yup. And now even my Wonder Worm days are over."

"Forever?"

I looked at Goog and smiled my wormy smile. "Nothing is forever, Goog." Then I groaned. "But the worm is definitely on hold. My mom gave me a non-stop thirty-minute lecture on being responsible, blah, blah, blah, blah, blah, blah, and my dad says I have to be nice to the Squirt and like it—or else."

"Or else what?"

"I didn't ask."

"Good thinking." Goog straddled the rail and swung his legs. "I never ask what that means either. The look on my dad's face when he says it always makes me think I don't want to know and don't want to find out."

"Well, the 'or else' couldn't be any worse than what they have me doing already," I said. "Goog, Goog, Goog! I've played at least twenty games of Candyland already and I bet a hundred of Uncle Wiggly—and the summer just started! Eesh. I've been stuck in Lollipop Woods and caught by the Bad Pipsisewah for the last three days. And all with a broken body!"

Goog shook his head. It was pathetic, all right.

"Wait. Wait," I said with a shiver. "The worst part is, I'm beginning to think those games are as much fun as Jonathan thinks they are . . ."

"Elliot! This is serious," said Goog with a shoulder shiver of his own.

"No kidding. I'm playing Chutes and Ladders, too!"

"Aaaaaaaaah!"

My summer was ruined, it was a disaster! A catastrophe! Everybody knows the only time having a broken arm is worth anything is during school when you can get out of stuff. I didn't want to get out of stuff. This was summer vacation. The first swim meet was only two weeks away. Now I'd be lucky if I even got to smell the chlorine all summer. And it had been the best season of my Little League career. Ever. I was hitting .350 for sure! Now I couldn't play ball. Couldn't go swimming unless my arm looked like a hoagie. My mom had me doing housework . . . *and* . . . I was baby-sitting Jonathan!

"At least there's one good thing . . . ," offered Goog.

"What?"

"It can't get any worse. What else can happen, right?"

We both started to laugh. Then I stopped. My toe started to tingle. My crooked sideways-facing little toe. The Alcorn Toe. The weird one only Grandpop, Uncle Jack, Aunt Clara, and I have. It was tingling, all right. And no good ever comes of a tingling Alcorn Toe.

"Uh . . . You don't really think it could, do you, Goog? I mean, get worse."

"Worse than this? Nah. No way." He laughed again.

"Right. No way." I laughed, too. Sort of. Kind of. But The Toe was still tingling.

Goog knuckle-knocked my cast. "At least it's a good color, Elliot."

I suppose the green slug didn't really look too bad. Last year when Pammie Lee Jordan broke her leg, the color of her cast was a disgusting yellow. Luckily mine didn't look like that.

"It sort of glows in the dark, too," I said.

"Glow-dacious!"

"Yeah, I checked it out last night under my covers."

Goog wiped his forehead with the end of his T-shirt. "Covers? You mean sheets, quilts, blankets? You're lucky you have air-conditioning. I won't even be wearing pajamas in my house until Christmas. My mom pulled the plug on all the air conditioners. She says she doesn't want to be responsible for destroying the ozone layer."

Goog's mother was a serious environmentalist, even in one-hundred-degree heat. She recycled things that nobody else even knew were recyclable. Goog says his mom has been washing aluminum foil and hanging it up to dry since he was wearing diapers. And I know for sure that she has the biggest ball of string in the world right there in her kitchen closet. I've seen that with my own two eyes. I don't know why anybody would want all that string, but if anybody ever does, Goog's mom has it.

"What did your dad say about no air-conditioning?" I asked.

"He told me to think cool."

Goog's dad was always telling him stuff like that. Thinking is his job. He works in a think tank. I used to think that meant Mr. Gugliocello sat in something like a giant fish tank all day, but Goog says it just means he thinks up new ideas and stuff. Like telephones where you see the person you're talking to and refrigerators and stoves that talk back. My dad is a lawyer. He doesn't think up any new ideas. He says he has enough trouble working with the old ideas some-body else thought up.

"Does thinking cool work?" I asked.

"Not too good." Goog squinted into the sun and wiped his forehead again. "I keep telling my brain to think cool, but my body keeps thinking sweat."

My body was thinking the same thing. It was hot, all right. The temperature had to be around ninety. This was the third day straight. We were baking.

"You know, Goog, you don't have to hang around here with me and sweat. Why don't you go on over to the pool."

"No, no. I'm okay. I'm practicing thinking cool. Besides, we have a game on Friday with the Giants. Joey Capelletti's on that team, remember? He's pretty tough. I don't want to wear myself out or anything."

"But Goog . . . today's only Tuesday."

"I know."

Good old Goog. Sweating a whole three days more than he had to. What a friend. Yup. I could always count on the Goog.

I stared at my glove, which was lying at the bottom of the stairs. "Hey, watch out for Joey's curve. It's a killer. He always strikes me out on that pitch. And Jimmy Gallagher plays a deep third. Goog, you know, I bet you could lay down one of your great bunts and beat it to first before he even blinks."

"I think you're right. I'm going to try that." Goog scratched his head. "Elliot, why don't you come to the game on Friday anyway? You could still sit on the bench with us."

"Do you think so? You think I could?"

"Sure. You're still one of us, even with the bad wing."

Yup. Goog was the best, all right. We looked at one another but didn't say anything. Then we stared into the hot sun and sweated.

Just the two of us.

"Ooh, Elliot—" Goog said as a sweat ball dropped off his nose. "I almost forgot! Did I tell you that Mrs. Kolosinsky moved yesterday?"

Mrs. Kolosinsky was Goog's next-door neighbor. She was the greatest. She always gave us her leftover Halloween candy—even before it got all stale and sticky. And I don't think she did that just because Goog and I shoveled her sidewalks and driveway when it snowed, either. She liked us anyway.

"Boy, she really got all teary and everything when she came over to our house to say good-bye."

"Did you?"

"A little. Nothing ran down my cheeks, though. . . . And Mrs. Kolosinsky said she told the new people moving in about us and hoped they would still let us use the basketball hoop over the garage."

Mrs. Kolosinsky always let us use the hoop. She even brought us something to drink when we were thirsty. Yes sir, Mrs. Kolosinsky was one great next-door neighbor.

"So who's moving in?" I asked.

"Don't know. Mrs. Kolosinky was sort of blubbery so nobody asked too much about them. All I know is that they have a dog."

"I hope it isn't some barking ball of fur like the one Mrs. Luppesscu has over on Elm Street."

Goog shook his head. "No, a real dog. Mrs. Ramsey from across the street said she saw somebody the other day from her living-room window walking around the property, and they had a dog with them. In fact, my mother said Mrs. Ramsey was sort of scared because the dog was big and mean. She said it looked like a wolf."

"A *wolf*?"

"That's what Mrs. Ramsey said."

"A dog that looks like a wolf . . . or a real wolf?" I held Goog's shoulders and stared into his eyes. "You know what a wolf means, don't you, Goog?"

He gulped. "Wow! Double wow. Do you think, Elliot? Do you really, really think?"

"Vampires," we whispered together.

"A vampire for a next-door neighbor! Is that cool, or what?" Goog shouted, jumping off the railing. "Hey, you know something? The moving van pulled up in front of the house just before I came over here. Want to go over to my house and check it out? We can watch them haul in the coffins."

"Excellent. Let's go." I stopped and held Goog by the arm. "But we can't let them see us. We have to be careful. *Very* careful."

"Right. Right," said Goog. "We're walking, talking blood bait." Goog snapped his fingers. "Hey, I know, we can spy on them from my bedroom window. They'll never see us from up there. And I'll borrow my dad's binoculars. We'll be able to see everything."

Vampire Busters. Maybe the summer wouldn't be so bad after all.

I opened the back door a crack and called out, "Hey, Mom . . . going to Goog's," before the screen door banged closed.

Goog pulled up the sweat socks that were hanging around his ankles, and we ran across the lawn.

The back door opened and the screen door squeaked. "Elliot . . . wait a minute now. Elliot?" Goog and I stopped at the edge of the driveway. We turned. There was Mom standing on the deck. "Elliot."

"Mom?"

"Take Jonathan with you, please."

I groaned. "Mo-om."

"El-l-iot."

I didn't even bother to try with another Mom, Mo-om, or Mo-o-om. It was no use. I knew the tone. Either Jonathan goes with us, or I don't go with Goog. The back door swung open and you-know-who ran out. I looked at Goog and nodded. "Yup. He's still here. This makes three days straight. Seventy-two hours . . ."

"How come?"

"My sister is at the doctor's again. My mother says Caroline says this is the day."

"Day for what?"

I made a face. "The *new* baby. Can you believe it! I'm going to get stuck with another one. As if having Jonathan around isn't bad enough."

"I thought that baby thing was last week."

"False alarm," I said as Jonathan hurried down the steps and came running toward us. "Of course, if I was this baby and knew I was going to be related to Jonathan, I wouldn't be in any hurry to get here either." Goog laughed. He could afford to laugh. He was no way near being an uncle to a squirt, baby squirt, or anybody else.

"Hi, Elliot. Hi, Goog." Jonathan turned and waved to my mother, and we headed up the driveway. "Uh . . . uh, Elliot?"

I stopped and sighed. "What?"

He stood on his tiptoes, leaned close to me, and

whispered, "You don't have to hold my hand."

"Don't worry. I have no intention of holding your hand! I only have one good one left and I'm not going to waste it holding yours. Just walk next to the curb and keep quiet, okay? And no singing or skipping. This isn't *Sesame Street.* Got it?"

He untiptoed and nodded. "Got it, Elliot."

"Good." We ducked under a low-hanging tree branch and turned up the sidewalk. Jonathan raised his hand. "What are you doing now?" I asked.

"I want to ask you if I can say something."

"Yes, Jonathan. You can say something." We stopped walking, and I looked over at Goog. Torture. Sheer torture. My mother was torturing me even with a broken arm. "Okay, okay, so what do you want to say? And make it quick. Goog and I haven't got all day."

Jonathan looked up at me. He smiled. "Just, thanks."

"Thanks? Thanks for what?"

"For taking me with you to Goog's."

I looked at Goog. Goog looked at me. Four-year-olds.

"Oh, come on, you little squirt." I put my arm around his shoulder and steered him toward the street. "And keep next to the curb like I told you. I don't want you getting run over and turning into a road pizza or something."

My mom would have me hauling out the garbage for the rest of my life if that happened.

3
A BIG BLACK PIANO

"MY TURN AGAIN."

I nudged Goog with my good elbow and knelt down against the sill in front of his bedroom window. I batted a dead bug that was stuck to the screen. Fat, juicy bugs were vampires' late-night snacks. I didn't want Goog's bedroom window to be some kind of welcome mat for any bloodsucker.

Goog handed over the binoculars, and I held them up to my eyes. I looked out over the big tree branch, past the telephone wires that went to the street, and then focused in on the moving van. It was huge. The writing across the side said TransVan Lines. Trans . . . Van. Uh-huh. Oh, yes. Like Transylvania maybe? They were clever, all right. Very, very clever.

Th-thump. Th-thump. Th-thump thump.

"When is it my turn?" Jonathan asked, swinging his

legs back and forth from Goog's bed and hitting the footboard with his sneakers.

"You don't get one," I answered.

Th-thump. Th-thump. "How come?"

"You just don't, that's all."

"And you don't want one, either," Goog said. I turned around just as he pushed a pillow behind his head. "Well . . . nothing is going on down there, Elliot. I think we're wasting our time. I hate to say it, but I don't think there are any vampires moving in next door."

"What are you talking about? *You* were the one who said they had a wolf."

"No I didn't. I said my mother said Mrs. Ramsey said they had a dog that *looked* like a wolf."

Same thing.

I turned back to the window and lifted the binoculars. I zeroed in again on the truck and counted another six chairs and two lamps as the movers took them off the van and carried them through the open front door. So far it was chairs: twelve; lamps: three; and coffins: zip.

"Well, I haven't seen any mirrors yet," I said. "Now

that's a sure sign of vampires. They don't make a reflection, remember?"

"I saw one," Goog said from under a tented comic book. "A great big one with ugly gold curlicues all over it. So much for sure signs."

"Well, they still could be vampires. Maybe that mirror is to fool regular people." I turned to Goog. "Like their neighbors. . . . Vampires are tricky, you know. They only come out at night, remember? It's only three-thirty. It's too light for them to show their faces now."

"And too hot," said Jonathan.

Goog laughed.

"Vampire Busters like us don't care about the heat, Jonathan," I said, wiping sweat from my nose.

Th-thump. Th-thump. Th-thump thump. "Elliot? Elliot?"

"Jonathan, stop bothering me. I'm on spy watch. I have to concentrate. And stop with that kicking already."

"But I have to ask you something," he said.

"Okay, okay. Ask. Ask. Quick."

Jonathan stopped thumping and cleared his throat.

"Well." He took a big breath. "How-come-we-have-to-spy-up-here-in-Goog's-room-and-sweat-when-we-could-spy-outside-under-the-tree-and-be-cool?"

Goog laughed again. I spun around and gave him another look.

"Well, when the Squirt's right, the Squirt's right." Goog rolled off the bed and fanned his face with the comic book. Then he fanned it over the turtle tank. Poor Herman looked like he was sweltering even in the water. It probably felt like a turtle hot tub in there. "I agree with Jonathan. I say we spy outside for a while."

I stood up and took the binocular strap from around my neck. "Okay, okay. Fine with me, if that's what you want. . . . But don't say I didn't warn you when late tonight you hear something squealing and scratching at your window and it turns out to be a creeping bloodsucker swooping over to you because he 'vants to drink your blood!'"

"*Aaahhhhhhhh!*"

"*Aaaahhhhhhh!*"

We chased one another from Goog's room and down the stairs. I jumped the last three steps, but

Goog beat me and Jonathan out the front door and across the front lawn. We all fell to the ground, and the grass felt good even if it wasn't much cooler than the ninety degrees it was everywhere else.

"Now can I have a turn spying?" Jonathan asked after he caught his breath. "Can I? Can I?"

Goog and I looked at each other. "Okay," said Goog. "But watch out they don't see you." He leaned closer to Jonathan and whispered. "Don't get yourself captured and turned into one of those vampire zombies."

"A vampire zombie?" Jonathan could barely whisper the words back. "What's a vampire zombie?"

"That's somebody who's had his blood sucked out when he wasn't looking," Goog said.

Jonathan blinked and gulped. I nudged him toward the other side of the yard. "Just be careful."

Jonathan hunched over and crept up to the hedge that separated Goog's house from the one next door. He looked back at us. "Go on . . . go on," Goog whispered, waving him on. Jonathan tiptoed closer to the bushes. He crouched down on his knees and spread apart some leafy branches to peek at the van. He stayed there for a couple of minutes and then came running back to us under the tree.

"I saw it! I saw it!" he puffed, trying to catch his breath.

Goog and I stood up. "Saw what? Saw what?" we said at the same time. Jonathan looked around to see if anyone was listening. He spread his arms as wide as he could. He took in a big breath and whispered, "A piano. A real big, black piano."

"That's it?" said Goog. "A piano?"

"Yup," said Jonathan, nodding up and down, back and forth. "Yup. Yup. Yup. I just saw three men carrying in a piano."

I looked at Goog. "Uh-oh . . ."

"Uh-oh what? . . . What?" he said.

"Girls. That's what."

"Girls?" he said.

"Girls. Pianos mean girls."

"They do?" said Goog.

"Practically one hundred percent of the time. Trust me."

"Are you sure, Elliot? I know—"

"Girls," I told him again. "Forget Count Dracula

and say so long to our vampire-busting summer. You're going to have girls living next door to you, Goog, my friend."

"Is that worse than vampires?" Jonathan asked.

"If they're anything like Grace and Peggy, it is." I laughed and leaned back in the grass.

"What are you talking about, Elliot?" said Goog. "You liked Elizabeth Mayerlink when she lived next door to you, and she was a girl."

"That's when I was two," I said. "Liking a girl doesn't count when you're only two."

Goog sighed. He knew I was right. Life as Goog knew it was over. "I wonder how old they are?"

"Who? The vampires?" asked Jonathan.

"The girls, Squirt, the girls," answered Goog. "Elliot, do you really think it's going to be bad—I mean really, really bad—living next door to a . . . girl?"

"I don't know what it's like living next door to one. I only live with them—and that's as bad as you can get."

Goog groaned. He looked terrible. Yup. Girls can do that to you, all right.

"But maybe having a driveway separating you helps," I offered as consolation. Goog still looked worried. "Oh . . . hey . . . who knows? Maybe it won't be that bad," I said, trying to make him feel better. "Jeffrey says sometimes having girls around is sort of nice."

"Really?" said Goog. "Your brother said that?"

"That's what he said."

"And he's in college. He must know what he's talking about, right?"

I shrugged. "Maybe. . . . Maybe other girls are not the same as sisters."

"I'm going to have a sister," Jonathan butted in. "Or maybe even a brother." He did a somersault on the grass. "Ta-da! Then I'll be the big brother in my family. Just like Jeffrey. . . . I'm going to be a big brother like Jeffrey, and my new baby brother is going to be the little brother. Like you, Elliot."

Goog let out a hoot.

"What's so funny?" I said.

"What Jonathan said."

"I don't think what he said was funny."

"Sure it's funny, Elliot. Don't you get it?"

"Get what?"

"When the new baby is born, Jonathan will be a big brother, but you'll always be a little brother. No matter how old you get, Elliot, you'll always be the baby brother."

"That's right," said Jonathan. "That's pretty funny, huh, Goog? Elliot will always be the baby brother."

"It's not that funny," I said. "I don't think it's funny at all." I pointed at Jonathan. "And you won't be laughing once that new little squirt starts pestering you like you pester me."

I don't know what was so great all of a sudden about being a big brother. I could have been a big brother myself . . . if I hadn't been born last.

Goog and Jonathan kept laughing and laughing and then started rolling around on the grass. They were wrestling! Goog looked like he was actually having fun with the Squirt. The heat was definitely getting to him. His brain was roasted.

With Goog's brain busy broiling, and the Squirt acting like the Squirt, I was of course the only one to see her walking around the hedge. A girl. Just like I'd told them. A piano-playing girl with red curly hair and earrings that looked like butterflies. And sunglasses. Pink sunglasses. Pul-ease!

Poor Goog. No driveway was going to be wide enough to protect him from a girl like this. When you have three older sisters, you get an icky feeling about stuff like that. Poor, poor, Goog. His summer was going to be as bad as mine. Maybe even worse!

The girl slid the glasses down her nose and looked at me.

I felt a tingling in my Alcorn Toe. Uh-oh. Worse than I thought.

"I'm Corinne Morrisey. I'm your new neighbor."

"Not *my* new neighbor," I said.

Goog looked up at the girl and suddenly stopped wrestling Jonathan. He got up off the ground and brushed blades of grass from his shirt all the while staring at her with a goofy-looking grin. "No, no—I'm your new neighbor. I mean, you're my new neighbor. I'm Goog, I mean, Phillip, I mean . . . Hi."

Phillip? What was with the "Phillip"? Mrs. Kolosinsky lived in that house for eight years, and he was never "Phillip."

"I'm nine. Are you nine? You look nine. I live here."

He pointed to his house. "He"—Goog pointed to me—"he . . . he . . . he lives somewhere else."

Somewhere else? What was the matter with him? Jonathan must wrestle better than I thought. Goog was acting like his brains had been rattled the way he was blabbering.

"I live around the corner," I said. "I'm his best friend, Elliot. I'm nine, too."

"Uh-huh," said the girl with a totally uninterested nod. "I'm practically ten."

"Ten! Wow," said Goog.

Wow? What was with the "wow"? So she was almost ten. Big deal. I was nine and a half. That was "practically" ten, too.

She pointed to my arm. "Is it broken?" She didn't wait for me to answer. "I broke my arm two years ago when I fell off my skateboard—"

"Skateboard!" interrupted Jonathan, getting into the act. "Did you hear that, Elliot? She can ride a skateboard. . . ."

I'd heard her say she'd fallen off a skateboard.

"Elliot broke his arm jumping off the deck where he wasn't supposed to be jumping and now he can't swim or play baseball or do anything but itch," Jonathan babbled before I could get a hand over his motormouth. "He's pafectic, aren't you, Elliot?"

"Pafectic?" said the girl.

"He means pathetic," I translated. "And I'm *not* pathetic."

"Uh-huh." There was that nod again. "I didn't think having a broken arm was such a big deal," she said with a shrug.

No big deal? No big deal? Get her. Of course it's no big deal when you do nothing but dopey girl things all day. It's a big deal when you play ball and are on the swim team. Of course it's no big deal when all you do is wear pink sunglasses.

"I didn't even cry," she said.

"How about that, Elliot?" said Goog. "She didn't cry, either!"

Like I cried? Who said I cried? Nobody said I cried.

"You must be brave. Real brave, right, Goog? Right, Elliot? . . . I'm Jonathan. I'm—"

"He's with me," I interrupted. There was no way this girl with red hair, pink sunglasses, and a skateboard had to know that I was the Squirt's *uncle*. Don't ask me why, but my tingling toe told me that was exactly the kind of information someone like this girl had no business knowing. Ever.

Jonathan folded his arms in front of his chest and nodded. "Yup. Elliot told us you'd be a girl, all right. But I was the one who saw the piano."

"Piano?" The girl didn't have a clue what Jonathan was talking about.

Jonathan nodded. "Elliot says pianos mean girls."

Of course. A brilliant bit of detective work on my part, if I do say so myself, but this girl didn't even have the manners to congratulate me.

Jonathan walked up to her and gave her the once-over. "So, do you sleep in a bed or in a coffin? We've been looking for the coffins." He turned to me and whispered, "But she doesn't look like a vampire, Elliot. No fangs."

The girl looked right at me and made a face. I couldn't believe it. This girl actually made a face at me! Whew. I felt sorry for the Goog having to live next door to *her.* She was even worse than Grace and Peggy combined. And that's as worse as you can get.

"Did you come from Transylvania?" Jonathan said

while circling. "That's where all the vampires come from, right, Elliot?"

I laughed. That was definitely a good one, even if it had come from the Squirt.

Goog didn't even smile. His face looked like it did in school when he tried to come up with an excuse for not doing his homework. "Jonathan means where did you used to live?"

The girl turned away from me and told Goog that her father just got transferred from his job. "We used to live outside of Atlanta, Georgia."

"Ahhh," I said. "So that's why you talk like that."

She stared. Goog stared. I wasn't too sure, but I think even Jonathan stared.

"What did I say? . . . What did I say?"

"Elliot just meant we could tell you weren't from New Jersey. Didn't you, Elliot?"

That's not what I meant at all.

"But what about your wolf?" Jonathan asked, still circling. "Don't you even have a wolf?"

"A wolf?" There she was, staring at me again. Like I was the one who said she had a wolf. "No-o. I don't have a wolf. I have a dog."

"A dog? Just a dog?" said Jonathan, sounding very disappointed. "Are you sure?"

"I'm sure. Just a dog. Her name is Pudgie, and she's a big, fat old beagle that can barely waddle."

"Pudgie?" Goog said to me.

"Beagle?" I said back to Goog.

He shrugged. "I guess Mrs. Ramsey wasn't wearing her glasses." Then he laughed. She laughed. Jonathan laughed. I didn't see what was so funny. In fact I didn't see why the Goog was even wasting his breath talking to this Corinne person at all. There he was, yapping on about this. Yakking about that. I didn't get it. Had to be the heat.

"Well, I guess I better be going," she said as Goog sputtered to a stop. "We have a lot of unpacking to do. I better get to it."

I grinned. Finally. Good-bye. Adios. Sayonara. Hasta la vista. Tootle-loo. GO.

"I just came over to say hello to my new neighbor and be neighborly." She turned from me and smiled at Goog.

Oh, brother. As if I even cared if she said hello to me. Get real, neighbor girl.

"Bye now." She waved, and ran across the yard. "Be seeing y'all."

Right. Wanna bet? Reality check, please! Like the Goog and I would want to see any more of her than we had to.

"Sure. Great. See you around," Goog called back.

I did a one-eighty. Did I just hear that come out of the Goog's mouth? "Sure"? "Great"? What was the Goog talking about? His brain was definitely broiled. No doubt about it. Broiled. Fried. Toast. All that sweating must have de-googified him.

"Hey, Corinne," he shouted. "Welcome to the neighborhood." Goog grinned as she disappeared behind the hedge. He looked at me. "So, what do you think?"

"Think? Think about what?" I said, wondering if his cheeks were beginning to hurt from all the smiling he was doing.

"Her."

"Her?"

"Corinne, Elliot. My new neighbor."

I shrugged. "She had an ugly-looking scar on her knee."

"Yeah. I thought that was cool, too."

"I didn't say that was cool. I just said she had a scar."

"Of course it was cool, Elliot. Scars are definitely cool. I wonder how she got it?"

"Who cares?" I mumbled.

"And did you hear her say 'y'all'? That's how people from the South say 'you all.'"

"I know that. Everybody knows that. Didn't I say that?"

"I like the way she says 'y'all,' don't you?"

"Eh. If you like that sort of stuff. . . . Hey, I have an idea. Let's go and—"

"Y'all," Goog interrupted. "You know something, Elliot? Piano and all, I think Corinne is going to turn out to be a pretty good next-door neighbor."

I thought vampires would have been better.

4

TEA BAG

WELL, MY MOTHER WAS WRONG, my sister was wrong, the doctor was wrong. Yesterday was not the day. It wasn't the night, either. The baby still didn't come . . . and Jonathan didn't go. He stayed the night. Again.

My sister kept saying the baby would be coming any time now. All I kept thinking was what my teacher Mrs. Hagabaum told us last year about elephants. She said it takes an elephant almost two years to have a baby. If my sister Caroline was anything like that, Jonathan was going to be here until next February. I'd probably be dead by then. Being nice to Jonathan twenty-four hours a day was killing me.

Of course, if the Squirt didn't get me, the heat

would. It was ninety degrees again. That made almost five days straight. I didn't care how silly I looked, I decided to go to the pool with my sisters and Jonathan even if I had to be wrapped in plastic and have an arm that looked like a submarine sandwich. Anything was better than staying home, sweating, and being unwormy to Jonathan.

"Grace, I'm sweltering in here," I said from the backseat of Mom's old Volvo station wagon as we pulled out of the driveway. "Put on the A/C."

"It's on. It's on. Give it a minute, will you, Elliot? Jonathan, are you wearing your seat belt?"

He patted the straps across his shoulder and waist. "Yup."

"Put the blower on," I said, already dripping.

Grace looked at me in the rearview mirror. "Elliot, I know how to drive."

"Turning on air-conditioning doesn't have anything to do with driving. It has to do with sweating. You may know how to drive, but I know how to sweat."

"Oh, stop your complaining, Elliot," said Peggy, who then had the dumb idea of singing "Old McDonald Had a Farm" all the way over to the pool.

Ten minutes of Jonathan cluck-clucking in my ear. And believe me, the kid cannot carry a tune. Torture. Total torture.

By the time we got to the pool parking lot, I was sopping wet and practically deaf in my right ear.

"Everyone have their badges?" Peggy said, hopping out of the car and walking around to the tailgate. I climbed out and put as much distance between them and me as fast as I knew how.

"Elliot! Wait up! Elliot!" yelled Grace as I was almost to the pool entrance and this close to a perfect getaway. "Wait for us! And come back here and help with some of this stuff."

Sisters. A broken arm and they made me carry a chair and three towels. I had to hold my badge between my teeth.

"Right here," Grace ordered as we walked around to the other side of the pool. "This is a good spot to put the chairs and blankets."

I spit out the badge and groaned. "This is by the baby pool."

Peggy kicked off a flip-flop. "It's the intermediate pool. And this is where we're staying so we can keep an eye on Jonathan."

Sure. Keep an eye on the lifeguards, she meant. She and Grace opened their lounge chairs and spread out their towels. Then they started slobbering themselves with suntan lotion. They even oiled the Squirt. Grace finally finished greasing up Jonathan and he slid off into the water. I don't think he even got wet. The water probably just rolled off his back.

"Now let me do you, Elliot," Grace said.

"No way. You're not doing me. I'm not smelling like some coconut."

"You have to wear sunscreen, Elliot."

"Do not."

"Do, too."

"Do not."

"Do, too."

"Do not."

Word war with my sister was almost as good as with Jonathan.

"Okay. So burn. I guess you've forgotten about that pair of blister epaulets you got two summers ago."

Well, almost as good.

"But before you turn into one big, ugly boil, get

over here and let me wrap your arm or you're not going in the water. And that is a direct quote from Mother."

Yeesh. I had to stand there next to her and Peggy, in front of tons of people, while the two of them oiled me anyway and wrapped me with plastic.

"Pink?" I shouted as Peggy started rolling it around and around my cast. "Do you have to use pink?"

"Oh, will you shush. That's all Mom had in the cabinet."

"I'm not wearing pink! No way."

"Fine." She dropped the roll. "It's this or nothing."

Sisters. They were just as bad as squirts. "Okay, okay, you already have me smelling like an Almond Joy, so, what's the big deal about wearing pink, I guess. But, no more. You've used enough already." She picked up the roll of plastic and kept wrapping. "Hey, I said that's enough! You're not wrapping a mummy. What are you using? The whole box? Be a little ecologically responsible, why don't you."

"Wait a minute," said Grace before I could pull away. "I have to put on this, too."

"Now what?"

She held up one of those freezer bags where my mother stores roast beef. I groaned as she made me slip my arm through a freezer lock bag with a hole at the other end. Then Peggy tied it up with rubber bands. If the rest of my body wasn't attached, my arm would have looked like a moldy piece of meat.

"This is embarrassing."

Grace lowered her sunglasses and whispered in one of her queen-of-mean whispers, "Do you want to go in the water or not?"

The sweat was pouring down my face, not to mention what was going on under the ol' pits. So what was so bad about being embarrassed?

"Elliot! Hey, Elliot!"

"Goog!" I shouted back as he waved and weaved around lawn chairs and blankets.

He dropped his towel and looked at me and my moldy arm. "You can't swim with all of that on, can you?"

"I can dunk."

"You mean you're going to be a tea bag?"

A tea bag is what all the kids at the pool called the adults who went into the water and didn't swim, but just bobbed up and down.

"A real Lipton Flo-Thru."

We laughed and headed for the big pool. Goog cannonballed in from the side. I had to walk down the steps with everyone looking at me and my pink plastic wrap. A tea-bag lady with a polka-dot bathing suit and frizzy hair sort of smiled, and a kid with braces laughed, but I didn't care. The water felt great. The chlorine smelled even better. The pits were happy, and I was cool.

Goog swam up from behind me. "Where's Jonathan?"

I pointed to the intermediate pool. "The three-footer. This one is over his head. This is about the only place since yesterday that I've been without him, not counting the bathroom."

Goog laughed. He could laugh. He wasn't an uncle. He wasn't even a brother. He was an only child. I think Billy Zakian said those kids had it made, too. We heard a splash and then a lot of clapping.

"It's coming from over there," Goog said, pointing to the diving board. "Somebody must have made a good one. I wonder who it was?"

I was pretty sure it was Paulie Martin. He does great jumps. He does a perfect Colorado. His splashes go clear out to the yellow letters on the cement. But it wasn't Paulie Martin. "Oh, no. How did she get here?"

"Who?" asked Goog.

"Her. . . . That . . . that . . . Corinne person."

Goog squinted and cupped his hand over his eyes. There she was, climbing up the ladder to the high dive. She walked out onto the board and curled her toes on the edge. "You're right. It's her. It's Corinne. My new neighbor. How about that, Elliot? That diver we heard everyone clapping for must have been Corinne."

No way. The board sprang as she jumped, and we watched as she did a perfect headfirst into the water.

"Boy. She's good, huh?" Goog said. "Elliot? I said, she's good, right?"

"She's okay."

"She's good, Elliot."

"So she's good. . . . What are you doing?" I said as Goog started to wave. "What are you doing? What are you doing?"

"I want her to come over here. Corinne. Corinne!"

She saw us and waved back. She started swimming toward us. Great. I ducked under the water. Too bad I couldn't hold my breath as long as forever.

"Hi," she said when I finally popped up for air.

I spit a mouthful of water. "Hi."

"Boy, you're a good diver," said Goog. "You didn't tell us the other day that you were a good diver, too."

She whipped her long wet braid from her back. "Oh sure. I've been swimming since before I could walk. Diving right in. Swimming like a fish, my mama says. And, of course, I practice a lot, too."

"Of course," I said.

"I was on the swim team in the town where I used to live. I won a couple of trophies, as a matter of fact."

"No kidding? Wow, that is good," said Goog. Then he looked at me. "Elliot won a ribbon last year at one of the meets here, right, Elliot?"

"Two, Goog. I won *two* ribbons. One hundred meter," I said. "Freestyle *and* butterfly."

"You? Really?" She sounded like she didn't believe it.

"Yes, really," I said. "Ask anybody. Ask Goog. Ask . . ."

"*I* won the freestyle two years in a row. League championships. I've got loads of ribbons. Just boxes full of those silly things. Medals, too."

"Wow!" said Goog, losing his footing and almost slipping under water. "Medals, too?"

I was beginning to wonder if "wow" was the only word Goog knew. So the girl could swim. Big deal. That wasn't any reason to get all mushy and make a fool of yourself.

Corinne dog-paddled around us. "What do y'all want to do?"

I spit another mouthful of water. "We're doing it."

"Yeah," said Goog. "We're just hanging out. Getting cool. Elliot is tea-bagging it for a while."

"Tea-bagging?"

Goog couldn't wait to tell her all about tea bags. She, of course, thought that was just hilarious. Ha ha. She was still laughing when she looked at my arm and said, "Pink is my favorite color, too."

Whoa. "Pink—pink is not my favorite co—"

"You know, I've got an idea," interrupted Goog. "Why don't the three of us play Marco Polo?"

Corinne looked at me and smiled. "Sure. Marco

Polo is fun. Sort of. Or, why don't we . . . race?"

"Can't," I said, patting sluggo. "Arm, remember?"

"Right. Your, uh . . . arm." She giggled. "Hmm. Well, since all Elliot can do is bob up and down, how about if you and I race then, Phillip? It will be fun." She looked over at me. "More fun than being a tea bag."

Oh, brother. This girl was a total . . . total . . . worm! Worm?

The light bulb went off. Now I got it. Oh yeah. I had her number, all right. Psychology! That's what she was using on me. Well, this girl was in for it now, because if there was anybody who knew about wormy psychology—it was me, Elliot Alcorn. I looked over at her and grinned. She grinned back. What a sucker. Baited. Hooked. I was about to reel her in. No way could she beat the Goog. Not a chance.

I leaned closer to Goog. "Whip her."

We decided on two laps across the pool. I was the judge. Corinne and Goog climbed out onto the tile edge. I waved my good arm to clear the lane. I crouched down and whispered in Goog's ear. "She's shakin'."

"She is?" said Goog.

"Trust me," I whispered. "You know you're just about as fast as I am. This will be cake." I stood up. The two of them leaned forward. "Ready?"

"Ready," they both called out.

"On your mark . . . get set . . . go!"

They hit the water with a splash. Goog was ahead by at least seven strokes. . . .

"Go, Goog!"

Three strokes. . . .

"Keep going, Goog."

No strokes.

"Goog?"

Before it was all over, Corinne had him by half the pool. I guess the Goog's skinny legs just couldn't do it this time. Goog huffed and puffed as he touched the tile edge. Corinne grinned a dopey water-dripping grin. I was outwormed and had never even seen it coming.

"She was just lucky," I said to Goog.

"And fast," he said, still trying to catch his breath.

"She certainly is."

That didn't come from my mouth. I turned around. Jeff was squatting at the edge of the pool.

"Hi," he said to Corinne. "You know this walking submarine sandwich?"

That was me? What was my brother doing? Squat-down comedy?

"Sort of," she said.

"She's Corinne. My new next-door neighbor," said Goog.

"Hi, Corinne, Goog's new next-door neighbor. I'm Elliot's brother, Jeff. I'm one of the swim-team coaches here for the summer. I was just watching you. Clocked your last lap."

"You did?" I said. What did my brother want to go and do a dumb thing like that for?

"You clocked me?" Corinne said as the water lapped around her shoulders.

"Sure did. You're good." Jeff turned to me. "Elliot, she swam the pool length just about a half second faster than your best time."

"Wow!" said Goog.

That *was* the only word he knew.

Jeff looked back at Corinne. "Listen, we need a replacement on the junior team for Elliot, because of his arm. . . ."

She looked at me and grinned. Again with the grinning.

"We really need a top swimmer. I know this is short notice, but are you interested in taking Elliot's place on our roster?"

My place!

"Oh, yes! Positively."

My place!

"Jeff," Goog sputtered. "She's won lots of league championships, too. She's got all kinds of medals and trophies. Just ask her. Go on, ask her."

"Great. I will. Sounds like you're really going to save the season for us, Corinne."

Save the season. Oh, brother. That was a bit dramatic.

"Stop by the team room before you leave today, okay?" said Jeff. "We'll get you all signed up. Okay?"

"Okay," she said. "Thanks a lot, Jeff."

Oh, yeah. Thanks a lot, Jeff.

"Boy, are we lucky somebody like Corinne moved in next door to me, huh, Elliot?" said Goog.

Lucky, lucky, lucky.

5

BELLY BOMB

YOU'D THINK MY SISTERS WERE SCREAMING over something important, like a game-winning home run, and not just another little squirt. Or squirtlette.

"A girl!" screamed Grace.

"A girl!" screamed Peggy.

"Girls," shushed my mother. "Settle down. I'm on the phone with Peter."

Oh no. My brother-in-law. Not him again. This was only about the ninety-ninth time since the crack of dawn that he'd called. Every fifteen minutes he was phoning with baby updates. And when my mother wasn't talking to him, she was talking to every relative we had. Some I didn't know we had.

Jonathan scrambled up over the arm of the chair

where my mother was sitting to get to the phone. "I'm a big brother. I'm a big brother, right, Dad?" he kept yakking into the receiver.

I slouched down in the chair in the living room and covered my ears. What was this big deal about being a big brother? I didn't get it.

"Mom, ask Peter who the baby looks like," Grace said as my mother kept waving at her to be quiet.

Hope she didn't look like you-know-who.

"Ask him if she looks like me," said Peggy.

Whoa. That would be even worse than looking like the Squirt.

My mother hung up the phone and sighed. "Oh, what a day."

Mom had that right.

"What a glorious day!"

Were we talking about the same day?

"Well, Caroline is doing fine, the baby is fine, Peter is fine . . ."

"Fine," I said. "Fine, fine, fine. Could we eat now?"

"What's made you so cranky?"

"Cranky? I'm not cranky."

"You sound cranky."

"I'm not cranky."

"You probably got up too early, with all this excitement."

"I didn't get up early." I wasn't going to lose sleep over some baby. Or anybody else, either. Especially some new neighbor whose name maybe begins with *c* and who just wormed her way onto my swim team. Like I cared. Which I didn't. "And I'm not cranky. I'm hungry." I looked at Grace and Peggy. "Well, is there something wrong with being hungry?"

Grace made one of her sister faces at me, then turned to my mother. "Can we go to the hospital with you this afternoon, Mother? Can we? Can we see the baby?"

"Yes, you can all see the baby, but only through the nursery window."

"Oohhhhhhhh, only through the window?" my sisters moaned.

Those two were squirrelly. "I'm staying home."

My mother looked at me. "Yes, stay home with Jeffrey. And take a nap, Elliot. You are cranky." Yeesh. I was not cranky! "And Jonathan," my mother said, giving him a hug, "because you're the big brother, your daddy said you can come, too, and see Mommy and even hold the baby if you want."

"I can? I can hold her? Oh, boy!"

Oh, boy.

"The hospital calls it a sibling visit," my mother said.

"A sipling visit?"

"That's 'sibling.' With a *b*," I said. What a macaroni.

My mother looked at her watch and got up from the chair. She took hold of Jonathan's hand. "Well then, let's hurry and get ready so we can be on time for visiting hours."

"Uh, Mom? . . . Mom? . . ." I asked, following them out of the living room and into the hall. "What about lunch?"

"Oh, we'll have something at the hospital coffee shop."

"Me! What about me?"

She was already halfway up the stairs. "Well," she said, calling over her shoulder, "there should be some bologna that isn't too old in the refrigerator. You can have a sandwich."

Bologna. I hated bologna. I can't believe my own mother wanted me to eat practically green bologna. "Who's going to make it for me?" I called up to her on the second floor.

Mom looked over the railing. "What do you mean, who's going to make it for you? You know how to make a sandwich, Elliot."

I moaned and rubbed my cast. "My broken arm, remember?"

"Oh, Elliot. Really now. I think you can manage making a little sandwich."

And then she disappeared. It was like she didn't care if I ate or starved. And me, her own flesh and blood with a broken body. I hadn't even seen the littlest squirtlette in person yet and already she was causing me trouble.

The only good thing about this baby business was that while everyone else was at the hospital doing the goo-goo ga-ga routine, I was left at home with some peace and quiet. The Goog came over and we couch-potatoed all afternoon. And ate. And it wasn't green-bologna sandwiches, either. Just me and Goog and two and a half hours of cartoons, videos, and assorted junk food. We nuked three packages of popcorn, and what we didn't eat we threw at each other or the TV. That wasn't too much since we made it just the way we liked it, drenched with two sticks of melted butter and lots of salt. It was perfect.

I clicked the channels on the remote control. "I think I'm still hungry."

"Me, too," said Goog as we reached the bottom of the popcorn bowl. He swirled the last kernel around in what was left of the butter.

"Should we make some more?" I asked.

"We could eat the ones on the floor."

"They look sort of beat."

"Any more M & M's?" he asked, wiggling his hand into the bag.

"How about one of those mini pepperoni pizzas we saw in the freezer?" I said as Goog came up empty.

He rolled off the couch and headed for the kitchen with me. I opened the refrigerator and grabbed two more cans of root beer. Goog helped me punch in the tabs, and I slurped the foam as Goog microwaved the pizzas. Goog always cooked the pizzas. He said his grandmother told him cooking was in his blood because he's Italian. She must be right, because Goog never nuked a bad pizza. (Although, come to think of it, neither did anybody else I knew.)

I took a bite out of mine and strung out the mozzarella between my teeth. Goog did the same. "Mine's longer. I win on that one," I said, sucking in the long glop.

Goog ate the stringy cheese from his fingers and laughed. "You should see the way Corinne strings out the cheese."

I swallowed, but the cheese got stuck halfway down my throat. "You had pizza with—her? Goog! What are you thinking?"

Goog slurped his root beer. "My mom just invited the Morriseys over last night so we could all get to know one another better. After all, we are neighbors."

"You mean there's more to know about her?"

"Oh, sure. Tons more. Tons. Get this. Do you know that she can sink a basket from way past the drainpipe? That's *s* when we play horse. Honest. Nothing but net. Her father taught her how to play when she was three! Three! Incredible, huh? Can you believe it?"

No. I chewed my pizza crust.

"She told me that she can teach me a corner kick for soccer, too. She was the MVP on her town's traveling team last year. I tell you, Elliot, that Corinne is really something."

"Yeah. She's something, all right."

"She has her own computer, too. Right in her bedroom."

I gagged. "You were in her bedroom? Goog. In her bedroom?"

"It wasn't that bad, Elliot. It wasn't. Honest. Besides, it was just for a little while, when we were waiting for the pizzas to be delivered. We went over to her house and played some computer games. Her room is cool, too. It was Mrs. Kolosinsky's son's room when he was a kid like us. Corinne said she likes it just the way Mrs. Kolosinsky left it. Baseball wallpaper and everything. Is she cool for a girl, or what?"

I vote "or what."

"Anyway, we played some games and stuff before the pizzas came. We got them from Buena Pizza. You know the place, right? They put on lots of gloppy cheese and all the extras. I taught Corinne how to string the cheese like we do all the time." Goog wiped tomato sauce from his chin. He started laughing. "You should have seen her, Elliot. She didn't know how to do it at all."

"No kidding? She didn't know how to string out the cheese? Who doesn't know how to do that?"

Goog shook his head. "She got pretty sloppy. There was sauce all over her face and cheese and onions hanging all over her chin." I started to laugh with him. "Yeah, she was a real mess."

"Was it on her nose, too? Nostril cheese?"

Goog laughed. "It was everywhere, I tell you. Everywhere. You should have seen her."

I could just imagine her in her little pink sunglasses and butterfly earrings with pizza cheese dripping from her nose and—

"But . . . by her third piece, she got the hang of it," continued Goog.

I stopped laughing.

"You know what, Elliot?"

"What?"

"Jeff was right."

"Right about what?"

"Girls."

"Girls?"

"About girls being okay sometimes. . . ." Goog stuffed the last bit of pizza into his mouth and chewed. "Corinne is really okay, don't you think, Elliot? And you know what she told me? She told me that I'm her first best friend that's not a girl or a dog. How about that, huh, Elliot? Me, the Goog, being a best friend to a girl. Who would have thunk it?"

I burped.

"Holy schmolie!" he said. "That was even louder than mine usually are. Let me try one."

Goog burped seven times in a row. He always was the better burper. Except this time. It was an even dozen for me. I was still burping past eight-thirty. And it wasn't just from the pepperoni.

"Too many belly busters in there, huh, sport?" Jeffrey said, patting my stomach as he sat down next to me on my bed. All I could do was grunt. "I know how you feel. I've been on the other side of that green face myself. I had a few pigouts in my day, too. But at least you're not barfing your brains out, right?"

Was he trying to make me feel better? I double-grunted.

Jeffrey looked at his watch, then at himself in the mirror above my dresser. He smelled better than usual. That meant a girl. He always smelled better when he was going out with a girl. Although I can't figure out why he wanted to waste smelling good on one of those. I don't know why you'd want to waste smelling good on anyone.

All of a sudden I got goose bumps and shivers. I wondered if Goog was going to get weird like that over Corinne. He's eating pizza with her. Shooting baskets. He's even going in her room! What's next, The Goog smelling good? Now that was scary. Really scary.

I burped. I mean BURPED.

"Well . . . Elliot, if you make it through the night . . ." I heard my brother say.

Make it through the night? Was he serious?

"I'll see you tomorrow."

"Thanks." I think.

"So long, Dad," Jeff said, walking out of the room just as my father was coming in. "Got a date. Got to go."

"Not too late," Dad called back.

"Hi, Dad," I moaned.

"Feeling okay?" he asked, tapping my cast.

I sort of grunted that I did. He sat down on the edge of the bed and it rocked worse than a boat. "Have you taken the medicine your mother told you to?"

"The pink stuff?" I nodded as my stomach rumbled.

"That should make you feel better soon."

"Uh-huh."

"Did you see the new baby today?"

Ugh. I couldn't even get the words out. All I could do was shake my head no.

"She's pretty cute, I'll tell you."

"Don't all babies look that way?"

Dad laughed. He folded his arms and crossed his legs. "I suppose. But not this baby."

Oh, boy. Here we go again. Body-snatched. Grand-pod-pa. Heave-ho and pass the Pepto.

"Not all babies look alike. Like you, for instance."

"Me?" I said, holding my stomach.

"That's right. You certainly didn't look like any other baby."

"I didn't?"

"No, sir. I remember standing by that nursery window in the hospital and thinking you were the most special baby in there."

I let go of my stomach. "I was? I looked special?"

"Absolutely. Mom thought so, too. And we both thought you were very handsome."

"And I had the Alcorn Toe, too, right, Dad?"

"That's right. You were the only Alcorn since Uncle Jack to have the famous Alcorn Toe."

I smiled.

"Until today, of course."

"Huh?"

"Yup. How about that? That new little baby has the famous Alcorn Toe, too."

I rolled over. How was that even possible? The squirtlette's last name wasn't even Alcorn, and now she was weaseling in on my toe territory. Everybody was weaseling in somewhere. Somehow. Someway. My stomach groaned and gurgled, and I let go with another gigantic belly belch just as my mother came into the room, with Jonathan right behind her. He was dressed in the Batman pajamas he had worn the night before. He climbed up on the bunk above mine and started jumping.

"How's your stomach feeling, Ellie?" Mom asked as she stopped Jonathan on his third trampoline trick and made him lie down beneath the covers.

I let loose with another pepperoni lollapalooza.

"Well, you close your eyes and get a good night's sleep. I'm sure you'll feel better in the morning."

My mother thought the answer to everything was a good night's sleep. How did she think I was going to sleep, with my stomach grumbling louder than my dad's snores and the Squirt squirming right above me all night long? She tucked Jonathan tight beneath the covers and kissed him on the forehead.

"Do you want a tuck and a kiss, too, Elliot?"

I groaned.

"Well, I'll assume that's a no," she said.

Good assuming.

"Good night, fellas," my father said, switching off the light.

"Good night, my guys," my mother said.

I groaned again.

"Grammie? Would you say, 'Good night, big brother'?" Jonathan asked.

"Of course. Good night, big brother."

Groan number thirty-seven.

I listened to their footsteps down the stairs until everything was quiet except for a few stomach rumbles.

"Good night, Elliot," Jonathan whispered. "Good night, Elliot . . . Elliot?"

"I hear you. I hear you."

"But you're not answering me."

"Okay, okay, good night."

"Elliot?"

"What?"

"Pop Pop said you ate too much with Goog. Did you eat too much with Goog? Did you, Elliot?"

"Yes. I ate too much with Goog."

"Grammie said you're sick. Are you really sick, Elliot?"

"And getting sicker."

Jonathan was quiet. Then I heard him clear his throat. "Elliot? Are you asleep?"

"No, I'm not asleep. How can I sleep if you keep yakking?"

"Elliot?"

"Now what?"

"Did I tell you my sister has soft skin?"

Even a pillow over my head didn't stifle the sound of him.

"I touched her hands. Her skin is the softest thing I ever felt."

"Yes, yes. You told me." My stomach was grumbling again. "You told me, you told Grammie, you told Pop Pop. You told everyone. Her skin is soft. Good. That's good, Jonathan. Now let's go to sleep."

I heard him rustle the covers. Punch the pillow. He was sitting up. He was definitely sitting up. I closed my eyes tighter. I wished there was a way to squeeze your ears shut.

"She's strong, too," Jonathan continued. "You should see the way she holds my finger."

Yeesh. I rolled over and mumbled, "All babies can do that."

"They can?"

"Yes. Yes. Even you. Even you did that."

"I did?"

"You did."

"How do you know I did that?"

"I remember, that's how."

"You remember when I was that little?"

I pounded my pillow. "Yes, Jonathan. I remember when you were that little."

"How did I look?"

"What do you mean, how did you look? You looked little. Like a baby."

"Yeah," Jonathan sighed. "That's what my sister looks like, too. Real little . . . like a baby. . . . Elliot?"

"WHAT?"

"Did I tell you I held her?"

"Five times."

"But did I tell you I held her all by myself? I sat in a chair and I held her."

I stared up at the bunk above me. "So? Big deal. I held you when you were a baby, too."

"You did?"

"That's right. I held you lots of times."

"Really? You held me lots of times?"

"Of course. . . . Well . . . I am your uncle, you know."

"I know. . . . Elliot? . . . Are you an uncle to my sister, too?"

"Yup. I'm an uncle to both of you."

The room was quiet.

"Elliot?"

"Hmm?"

"Do you feel better?"

"I don't know. Sort of. I guess. Yeah. I do," I said through the dark. "My stomach even stopped grumbling. How about that? The pink stuff must be working. . . ."

"That's good. Good night, Elliot."

"Yeah, good night, Squirt. See you in the morning."

6

THUMB NOOGIES

THERE IT WAS. Right in the middle of the living room, for Pete's sake. This big white and pink *thing*. Ruffles. Bows. Hearts. Yuck.

"Isn't it adorable?" My mother had that grandmother look. And sound. She was cooing. Cooing at the thing.

I fell across the couch. "What is it?"

"It's a bassinet. It's where the baby sleeps, Elliot."

"I thought it sleeps in a crib."

"Elliot. Babies are too little to sleep in cribs when they first come home from the hospital. And stop calling the baby 'it.'"

"Well, what else am I supposed to call it?" I popped my gum. "Nobody wants to give *it* a name."

My mother fluffed all the white puffy stuff hanging over the *thing* and started stapling. My mother doesn't sew, she staples. Or tapes. If she ever gets to the point where she needs string, I'm going to send her over to Mrs. Gugliocello.

"We'll know her name tomorrow when Peter brings Caroline and the baby home from the hospital," Mom said as she banged along with her staple gun. "Caroline said it was a surprise."

Wasn't the baby enough? She had to come up with some dopey surprise, too? I sat up. "Wait a minute. He's not bringing them here, is he?" Just the thought of it almost made me swallow my Bazooka.

"Elliot, stop being difficult."

"Well, is he?"

"Of course not." She stapled another ruffle. "I'm just getting the bassinet ready for the nursery at their house."

I sighed. That was a relief. I leaned back on the couch cushion and put one foot on the coffee table. "Does that mean we'll be getting rid of Jonathan, too?" My mother gave me one of her looks. "I mean . . . is Jonathan going home?"

"Yes, Jonathan will be going home. And get those feet off the furniture," she said, tying another pink bow and letting loose with the staple gun again.

"We're ho-ome."

"Grace? Peggy? . . . Jonathan? Elliot and I are in here," my mother called. "Come see the bassinet."

"Oh, Mom," Peggy practically gasped, running over to it. "This is so adorable. Grace, look at the bassinet."

"This is so c-ute. It's so little and look at all the pink bows. I love it," Grace mushed. "But, wait until you see what we bought the baby." She dropped an armful of packages on the carpet. "Mom, Peggy and I found the sweetest little dress and a sweater with kittens on it and the tiniest romper . . ."

Baby clothes and yak yak. Get me out of here. I was two steps from a clean getaway when Jonathan yanked me by the hand. "Look what I got her, Elliot. Look what I got her." He started plowing through the bags and boxes. "Look, Grammie. Look, Elliot. Look at what I got for my new sister." He dug way down in one of the shopping bags and pulled out some white lump of a stuffed animal. "Look, Elliot."

I nodded. Big whoop.

"And look at this." Peggy held up a peanut-sized dress. "Isn't this the most precious thing you've ever seen?"

Yeesh.

I left them all *oohing* and *aahing* and went out to the backyard for some peace and quiet. Then my arm started to itch. I had my midnight-emergency stick under my bed, but there was no way I was going back in the house now, itch or no itch. I looked around the backyard and found a pretty good twig a few feet from the big oak by the side of the garage. I wiggled it under the cast and scratched.

"Hey, Elliot."

I turned. "Goog! Hey, what are you doing here? I thought the big game was tonight?"

Goog made an invisible swing. "It is. I came over to make sure you were coming."

"Are you kidding? Wouldn't miss it. Six-thirty, right? Henderson Field?" Goog nodded. "Remember to watch out for Joey Capelletti's curve. . . . And tell Zack Wilson to play deep against Gary Shapiro, and . . ." I squinted my eyes as I looked into the sun. The Goog didn't need me to tell him any of this.

"Ah, you guys will do great."

Goog drew a line in the dirt with his sneaker. "Wish you could be playing with us." I nodded and patted my arm. We didn't talk for a while. "So, uh . . . how's the . . . you know," said Goog.

"Oh. The baby?"

He nodded.

"Don't let this get around, promise?" Goog crossed his heart and held up his hand. "A girl. I'm an uncle to a girl now, Goog."

"That's bad, huh?"

Bad? It was terrible. Awful. Humiliating. How could the Goog even ask such a question?

"El-li-ot." My mother was calling from the back door. "Come on in here and see what the girls bought for you to give to the baby."

I winced. "I have to go, Goog." The Goog understood.

"I'll see you tonight," he called back, running down the driveway.

As usual, "you" turned out to be "us." But I made Jonathan promise no dumb questions or holding my hand in front of anybody I knew. I figured that wouldn't make hanging around with the Squirt too bad. Mom had totally embarrassed me already by calling Mrs. Gugliocello and asking her to "keep an eye" on us. (One minute she tells me I'm not a baby, and the other she's treating me like one. I don't get it.)

At least she trusted me with money. She gave me six dollar bills, and after Jeffrey dropped us off at the field around six o'clock so we could watch the guys take batting practice before the game, we went to the snack stand. We each got a popcorn and a frozen Snickers bar, which came to $2.50. I stuffed the change in my shorts' back pocket and steered Jonathan toward the bleachers and a good spot to watch the game.

Goog saw us right away, and I waved as he picked up a bat and took a few swings. Our manager, Mr. Anderson, even waved to me and then took the mound and pitched a few to Goog. First, he got off a rocket that flew past third base. Then he hit a pretty deep fly ball to center on another.

I cupped my hands around my mouth. "Good going!"

"Good going!" Jonathan called out.

Goog walked away from home plate and motioned for me to come down to the bench. He kept waving. I turned to Jonathan. "Listen, you stay here while I go talk to Goog for a minute."

"Can I eat your popcorn?"

"Yes, you can eat my popcorn. But you stay right here, understand?"

"Understand."

"No jumping off the bleachers. No talking to strangers. No going anywhere with anybody. Got it?"

Jonathan took the box of popcorn from my hand and munched a fistful of his own. He nodded. "Got it."

"And if you're good," I said, staring him in the eyes, "I'll get you an ice cream later."

"Yea! Ice cream."

"But only if you're good."

"I'll be good. When you're good, good things happen. Mommy told me that."

My sister Caroline was sounding more like my mother every day. Scary.

"Okay, so be good, and I'll see you in a little while. Remember, don't move."

I hopped down the bleachers to the dugout on the home side of the field. All the guys were there. Nicky Locastro, Billy Zakian, Zack Wilson. We did our team handshake—two thumb noogies and an elbow bash.

"Boy, Alcorn, are we missing you," said Billy as he patted me on the back.

"Really?"

"We lost two in a row since you broke your arm," said Zack. "Nobody plays shortstop as good as you do."

Goog straightened his cap. "Sit on the bench with us, Elliot. Mr. Anderson said it was okay. I already asked him. Come on, before the game starts."

I looked at all the guys in their uniforms, sitting there laughing. Talking. Spitting. Punching their gloves.

"Come on," Goog said again. "Sit down."

I turned and looked back up at the bleachers. "Hmm, I don't know. Jonathan is with me and . . ."

"Oh, he'll be okay. Practically everybody's mother is sitting up there. What could happen to him?"

"Nothing, I guess, but . . ."

"At least stay for batting practice."

"Well . . ."

"Elliot! Hey, El, come on down here," Danny Jacobus called out to me from the end of the bench.

"Arm looks good, Alcorn," Stevie Levin said as I squeezed in on the bench between him and Kevin Harris. He tapped my cast. "So when do we get to sign it?"

"Yeah, Elliot," said Goog. "When do we get to sign our names?"

"Let's do it right now," said Stevie. "It will be good luck."

"I've got a marker in my backpack," Kevin said, jumping off the bench and running to a pile of stuff at the end of the dugout.

"Here's a red one," Billy said, holding up another pen.

The guys took turns writing their names and funny junk all over the green monster. Kevin drew a neat-looking baseball and wrote *Hurting without you.* Nick drew my uniform number. He was just coloring in the seven when the Giants took the field for their warm-up. As we watched them take ground balls, we took turns spitting. Mikey Gries beat Goog by two inches.

"They don't look so hot," I said as the balls barely made it past second base. "You'll cream these guys."

"Hope so," said Zack. "Mr. A's got me playing shortstop, but I play better in the outfield. I hope I don't make any errors."

I patted his back. "Shortstop is no big deal. You'll do great."

"Thanks, Elliot."

Mr. Anderson started to head out to home plate with the lineup card. "I better get going. Game's about to start."

Goog took off his cap and scratched his head. "Are you sure you don't want to stay here and sit with us?"

"Mmm, I better go. . . . I sort of promised Jonathan that I'd buy him some ice cream." I gave Goog a thumbs-up and called to the rest of the team. "Good luck. . . . Mow 'em down, guys."

I turned and headed for the bleachers. I looked at my arm and the names written all over it. It looked great. It even felt great. I decided that I might even have an ice cream myself. There was just enough time

to go to the snack stand before the first pitch. I looked
up to the stands and started to wave for Jonathan to
come down.

But he wasn't there.

7

THE BLOODSUCKER

I COUNTED . . . FIFTH ROW, FOUR PEOPLE in from the middle aisle. That's exactly where we were sitting. Mr. Zakian had been on one side of us, and on the other, a man who was wearing a bright blue bowling shirt with the name Ray written on the pocket. Fifth row. Four people. I counted again. Jonathan still wasn't there. He wasn't where I left him.

"The little goof probably moved to another seat," I mumbled to myself, walking quicker. "I told him to stay put. I told him not to move," I kept mumbling. "Well, no ice cream for him. That's it. Absolutely no ice cream for him."

I looked all across the bottom row. The second row. The third. All the way to the top. The very last row.

He wasn't sitting in any of them.

He couldn't have fallen through the bleachers, could he? I was pretty sure one of those moms up there would have noticed something like that. I ran underneath the bleachers just to make sure. No. . . . No Jonathan lying around. I guess that was good.

But then, where was he?

I looked around the fence circling the field. There were two little kids hanging around by left field. One kid had spiky blonde hair. That wasn't him. Jonathan's hair could look pretty wild sometimes, especially in the morning, but the kid with spiky hair definitely wasn't him. Nobody was on the swings. Or under them. The slide, either. I checked that out, too.

So where was he?

He wasn't by the basketball court. Or the parking lot, either. Then my toe started tingling. Uh-oh. I started feeling sweaty. Clammy. I took a deep breath. Think, Elliot . . . think. Think. Think. If you were the Squirt, where would you wander off to? I mean, he had to be somewhere. Didn't he?

Then I smelled it. Not the Squirt. Hot dogs.

Food. Sure. That was it. He had to be where the

food was. He was always where food was. I raced over to the crowd around the snack stand. A whole bunch of people were calling out orders for hot dogs and sodas. But not Jonathan. I wiggled in between two mothers with baby carriages. No Jonathan. I squirmed past Eddie Bamberger's father, who was chewing on one of his smelly cigars. Still no Jonathan. I didn't get it. Here was the food . . . so where was the Squirt? Where was he?

I didn't want to go yelling and shouting his name all over the place. . . . It wasn't like he was lost or anything. . . . He wasn't lost. Right? He couldn't be lost. Right? He definitely wasn't lost. Right? Right! Right! Right! There wasn't any reason to go and start yelling all over the place. That's the kind of dumb thing my goofy sisters would do. . . . Start yelling. Screaming. . . . Acting hysterical. Like something was really wrong. Like something awful had happened to him. . . .

"Jonathan? . . . JONATHAN!" I could feel the veins on my neck bulging. "JON-A-THAN!"

"Elliot?"

I turned around.

There he was. Standing right by the old Coke machine. He was smiling. He was okay. . . . Well, almost.

He was with HER.

I knew something awful had happened to him.

"Jonathan, what are you doing over here?" I could still feel the veins in my neck pulsing. "I've been looking all over for you. Didn't I tell you to stay put?"

"Oh, please don't be angry with Jonathan," Corinne said before Jonathan could open his mouth. "It's really my fault he's over here."

Figures.

"I sat down on the bleachers next to him and we started talking and all. He said he wanted ice cream, and I did, too, so I just thought I'd get some for both of us."

"Chocolate," Jonathan said, licking the cone.

"Hey, didn't I tell you not to talk to strangers?"

"Corinne's not a stranger," said Jonathan.

No. She's just strange.

Jonathan leaned close to me and whispered, "I don't think she's a vampire, either."

Right.

Corinne smiled. "I'm sorry if I got you all scared, Elliot."

"*Scared?* Me? Who said I was scared? I wasn't scared."

"Oh. You looked sort of scared."

"I wasn't scared. I . . . I . . . I was just worried about where Jonathan was, that's all." The girl obviously knows nothing about responsibility.

"Hmmm . . ." She caught a drip from her ice-cream cone. "I thought maybe Goog told you I was in the bleachers and you would just put two and two together that Jonathan was with me. . . ."

"Goog? Goog knows you're here?"

"Invited me this morning right after I came home from the swim meet. I came in first. We beat North Harrington. Didn't your brother tell you?"

"He might have mentioned something about it," I mumbled.

"So, I guess Goog told y'all about the game, too?"

"Of course he told me. He told me this afternoon."

She licked her cone. "Oh. This afternoon. Just this afternoon?"

"He just *reminded* me. Heck, I knew when the big

game was. I'm on the team, remember?"

Jonathan slurped his cone. "Elliot, what's that writing all over your cast?"

"Oh, yeah. How about this? Looks pretty good, huh?" I held out my cast for Corinne to see. "The guys wanted to write their names and stuff on it for good luck."

"Good luck for who?" Corinne said.

"What do you mean, good luck for who?"

"Well, good luck for you or for the team?"

"For both of us. Good luck for both of us. Yeesh. That's what guys do on a baseball team. Wish each other good luck. We're friends. We're more than friends. We're a team . . . we're . . ." What was the point? This Corinne person didn't have a clue. "Oh, come on, Jonathan. Let's go find some seats before the game starts and you get lost again." I put my arm around his shoulder. "And watch it. You're dripping."

Jonathan kept licking his cone, and we squeezed past a group of mothers sitting in the fourth row. Unfortunately, we couldn't lose Corinne. She sat down next to Jonathan.

"Oh, there's Mrs. Gugliocello." Corinne pointed and waved.

"Hi, Corinne. Hi, Elliot. Hello there, Jonathan," called out Goog's mom.

"Mrs. Gugliocello is my neighbor," Corinne said.

"I know. I know she's your neighbor. She's my best friend's mother, remember? *I* call her Mrs. G."

"Here come the guys," Jonathan said as the team took the field.

"There's Goog," Corinne said, waving and clapping.

Jonathan sucked the last of the ice cream from the bottom of the cone and stuffed what was left into his mouth. He crunched and chewed and leaned closer to me. "Corinne told me she wants to be on the team," he whispered.

"What team?" I whispered back.

"That team," whispered Jonathan, pointing to the field.

"My team?"

Jonathan swallowed. "She plays shortstop."

I turned and looked at Corinne. "*I* play shortstop."

She brushed a red curl from her cheek. "Last season

I batted an even .300."

Jonathan wiped his chocolate mustache with the back of his hand. "Elliot was hitting .350 before he fell and broke his arm, right, Elliot?"

I gave him a pat on the back and smiled. "That's right."

"Three-fifty?" she said.

"Yup. I was having a pretty good year."

"You mean a pretty good *half* year."

"Huh? What does that mean?"

"That means who knows what your batting average would be if you played the whole season. . . . You know . . . slumps and all. . . . Maybe not even as good as .300. Like me."

"Shortstop?" I said.

"Shortstop," she said.

"PLAY BALL!" shouted the umpire. Corinne smiled and turned toward the field.

The old Alcorn Toe was tingling like crazy. Nobody was going to tell me this Corinne person wasn't a vampire. This girl was a bloodsucker, all right. No doubt about it. First it was the swim team. Then eating pizza with Goog. But shortstop? Shortstop?

This meant war.

I looked over at Corinne and grinned one of those great grins that took every one of my nine and a half years to perfect.

The Wonder Worm was back.

8

SQUIRTLETTE

JONATHAN AND I FINISHED OUR umpteenth checkers game of the night. I decided a couple of days ago to teach him how to play some games besides Uncle Wiggly and Candyland. If I had to be responsible, I figured I might as well be responsible doing something that *I* liked for a change. Jonathan was getting pretty good at Monopoly, too, which is my favorite, but he really liked checkers. He won the last four games we played. I let him. (Well, I let him win one, anyway.)

"Let's play one more," he said, spilling the checkers back on the bedspread.

"Jonathan, I'm tired. It's . . ." I turned and looked at the clock on the nightstand next to our beds.

"Whoa. It's after nine-thirty. We have to get some sleep."

And besides, I wanted some time to plan some diabolical worm-warfare strategy against Corinne before I got some shut-eye. Yessir. I was going to sweep the floor with that dust mite.

"But I'm not tired," yawned Jonathan.

"Well, you have to go to sleep anyway. It's your big day tomorrow, remember?"

He grinned and nodded. "My mom and new sister are coming home."

I grinned, too. They weren't the only ones going home. Finally.

I folded up the board and Jonathan gathered all the checkers. I put the game away on the top shelf of my closet.

"Hey, did you brush your teeth? You don't brush them and they're going to look like scum buckets, Squirt."

"Ooh. I forgot. Thanks, Elliot." He ran down the hall into the bathroom. I waited for him to finish brushing and listened as he made the last toilet pit stop for the night. The toilet flushed and Jonathan padded down the hall back into the bedroom. He climbed up the ladder into bed.

"Ready?" I asked, standing by the light switch.

"Ready," Jonathan said from under the covers. I flipped off the light switch on the wall and climbed into the bottom bunk.

"Yup. Tomorrow is the big day," I sighed, closing my eyes and thinking about ways to blindside Corinne. I just hoped all those days of Candyland hadn't rotted away the wormy side of my brain.

Jonathan sighed. Then he sighed again. And then I heard something that sounded like a sniffle. "Hey, you're not getting a cold are you?" That was all I needed now. Jonathan not being able to go back home because of a dumb cold. "You didn't catch anything from that Corinne person, did you? I told you not to get too close to her."

"No. I'm not getting a cold."

"Good. Well, go to sleep. Big day tomorrow. Big, big day."

Jonathan sniffled again. "Elliot? . . ."

Oh, brother. "What?"

"Nothing. I guess. But, well, uh . . . this is my last

night sleeping over here with you, huh?"

Jonathan was quiet. There was that sniffle sound again. Geez. I hope the Squirt wasn't going to start blubbering and bawling. . . . Then I'd never get any sleep.

"Nah," I finally said. "You'll be sleeping over here again."

"Really, Elliot? Promise?"

I sighed. Well, what else was I going to say if I wanted to get some sleep? "Well . . . uh, sure. Your mom and dad will be having Grammie and Pop Pop baby-sitting you for overnights lots of times."

"Really? Just like always?"

"Sure. Just like always." I couldn't believe those words were actually coming from my mouth. But they were. They were, all right. "Nah. . . . Having a sister won't change that."

I could hear the Squirt sigh.

I sighed myself.

"Elliot?"

"Uh-huh."

"I just want you to know that I don't think Corinne is as good a shortstop as you are."

"You don't?"

"No way. Not even close."

"Gee. Uh . . . thanks, Squirt . . . thanks."

There they all were, crammed in Caroline's living room fighting for the best positions by the windows to watch for my sister to come home. Well, not exactly my sister. The baby. The baby was the one they were waiting for.

My arm was itching and my stomach was grumbling. I left the "watch" and went into the kitchen to look for some food. My mother had enough pots rumbling on the stove to make anyone think it was Thanksgiving or something. Go figure.

"Elliot, get your nose out of those pots," my mother said, coming into the kitchen.

"I'm hungry," I said, dropping a lid.

"You can't be that hungry."

"Yes, I can," I said, leaning against the counter.

"Oh, stop." She wiped her hands on a dish towel. She kissed the top of my head. "Try to hang on just a bit longer, Elliot. We'll be having lunch as soon as they get here."

Oh, sure. I believed that one. I knew what was going to happen. By the time everyone stopped gooing and ga-ga-ing over the newest squirtlette, I was going to be on the verge of starvation.

"They're here!" we heard Peggy shout from the other room. "They're here!"

Stampede time for the door: my mother, Grace, Peggy, Jeff, and my mother's oldest sister, my aunt Katie. Luckily, Peter's family lived five hundred miles away or they'd be swarming around here, too. Unbelievably, my father was the first one out the door. Holding a video camera gives you first dibs, I guess. I watched from the porch as they all made a beeline for the car.

"Easy now. Take it easy," my mother kept saying as Peter helped Caroline out of the car. "How are you doing, Darling?" Kisses. Lots of kisses. Grace and Peggy had their noses pressed to the rear car window, looking at the baby. I wondered if they had acted this goofy when Mom brought me home from the hospital when I was a baby. That was pretty hard to imagine, even with a good imagination.

"Here she is, here she is," my father said as Peter

lifted what looked like nothing but a bundle of blankets from the car seat. "Let me get another angle of that. Pete, go back in the car and get out again."

I couldn't believe he said that. I couldn't believe everyone else thought it was a great idea.

"I'm a big brother," Jonathan kept yakking as he hopped around the front lawn like a rabbit.

The pack moved inside, still gooing, but quietly. "Don't frighten the baby. Babies are afraid of loud noises," my aunt Katie repeated every three seconds as they all huddled around the bassinet that was in the living room.

"Oh, let me hold that little darling," my mother gooed, before the baby's bottom even touched the bassinet. "Come here, Grammie's little baby. Come to Grammie."

"When do we eat?" I asked.

"Elliot." My mother was glaring her grandmother glare again.

"What?"

She didn't answer. She just turned back to the baby and started gooing again. Then everyone had to make sure Caroline was comfortable. Lots of pillows. Feet up. Of course, there was a battle between Grace and Peggy over who was going to hold the baby first. My mother had to referee. Grace won, because she was older. Peggy actually looked at the clock and timed how long Grace got to hold the baby. Photographs? Forget about it. There were enough flashbulbs popping to blind the poor squirtlette. What a way to spend Saturday afternoon.

"Okay, now let's have one with the mother, dad, son, and daughter," Jeffrey said, organizing the group, as my father continued to video everybody and everything. I watched him pan the bassinet at least three times, and the baby wasn't even in it.

"Say 'cheese,'" Jeff said as Jonathan and Peter huddled around Caroline.

I don't think my sister had seen herself in a mirror lately, because if she had there'd be no way she would have let anyone with a camera in the same room with her.

"You look beautiful," my mother told her.

My mom's eyes were definitely going. Too bad I hadn't brought my camera. I could have blackmailed Caroline for life. My stomach was grumbling again. I went back in the kitchen to see what I could scrounge. I picked up a carrot stick and crunched.

"Elliot? Elliot, there you are," my mother said, coming into the room. She picked up a dish towel that was hanging over the top of a chair and tied it around her waist. "Go in there. Go on, they're waiting for you."

"Why?"

"Because it's your turn to have a picture taken with the baby, that's why."

I groaned. "Do I have to?"

"Go," she said, pushing me out of the room before I could even think of a good excuse.

"Come on, Uncle Elliot," Peter said, nudging me toward the bassinet. "Let's get a picture of you two now. Sit down in the chair by the fireplace so it will be easy for you to hold the baby."

"Hold it!" Whoa. "Couldn't I just stand by that crib thing or something?"

"Oh, Elliot, just sit down already and hold the baby so we can get a picture, and then have dinner," bossed Grace.

Anything to finally get something to eat. I eased

into the green chair and held out my arms and waited.

"Not too stiff, Elliot," said Caroline as she lowered what looked like a bundle of blankets into my arms. "Watch your cast. That's it. Relax. Breathe, for heaven's sake, Ellie. Okay . . . you're doing fine. Support her head like this," she said, showing me.

I was holding her. Although it didn't feel like I was holding anything but blankets and a head. I guess she didn't weigh too much. She sure was little. Her face was sort of scrunched and red, and her hair looked like a bunch of feathers sticking all over her head.

"She's so beautiful," Peggy sighed.

Beautiful? She looked pretty funny to me. She smelled good, though. I put my nose to her head. Yup. She did smell good. I touched her hand. Jonathan was right. She was soft.

"Smile, Elliot," Peter said as he clicked away.

"I want one of the proud uncle, too," Aunt Katie said, elbowing her way beside Peter.

"Make it quick," I said between smiles. "She's starting to wiggle. . . . Hey, hey . . . help! She's opening her mouth."

"She's yawning," Grace said.

Caroline laughed. "You're doing fine, Elliot. She looks very content."

"She does?"

"Yes. She looks very happy in your arms."

I looked down at the pip-squeak. Maybe my sister was right. The baby did look like she was smiling.

"Watch how she holds my finger, Elliot," Jonathan said as he practically forced his pinky into her grasp. "See how she does it?"

"Yeah, yeah. She did that for me, too. But I think she's had enough of that for today. That's probably like exercise for her. Remember, she's only a baby."

"Right," Jonathan nodded. "Elliot, did you check out her toe?"

Oh yeah. The Toe. Caroline unraveled the blanket and pulled off the knitted sock with the pink bow.

"What do you know," I said, looking down at the little sideways toe. It looked just like mine. It really did look just like my own toe. How about that?

"Well, dinner is almost ready," my mother said, walking into the room. She looked at me and smiled. Then she turned to Caroline and Peter. "So, you two, when are you going to end the suspense and tell us what you named my granddaughter?"

Caroline grinned. "Peter and I decided that in honor of her uncle and *godfather*, Elliot . . ."

Elliot? Me?

". . . we're naming her Elyse. Little Ellie."

"Little Ellie. How wonderful," my mother and father said almost at the same time. "Elliot, isn't that nice?" my mother asked.

"Nice," I said, sort of nodding, although I wasn't sure if having a girl named after you was nice or not.

"So, tell us, Elliot. How does it feel to be an uncle and a godfather?" Dad asked. "Elliot? . . . How does it feel?"

I lifted the baby from my lap.

"Wet."

9

GO FISH

GOOG PUSHED THE ORANGE CRATE he was sitting on closer to me. He leaned across the cardboard box we were using for a table and stared into my face. "Any fives?"

I smiled. "Go fish."

The rain was just a spit now, even though a giant puddle was still growing near us right in front of the garage door. Jonathan pulled off his Nikes and tossed one of them in the wheelbarrow my father kept in the corner. I heard the second one hit the lawn mower. He peeled off his socks. (Goog and I smelled that move.) Then he ran outside and jumped in the puddle with a splash. He leaned his head back and stuck out his tongue.

"Look. I'm catching raindrops."

Goog and I laughed as we watched him catch the drops like he was going after pop flies.

"Come on, Jonathan. It's your turn," I called. The smell coming from an open bag of damp peat moss made me sneeze.

"Bless you, Elliot."

"Never mind blessing me," I said, scratching my nose with my good hand. (That kid could really be goofy sometimes.) "Just get back in here before you catch cold."

Jonathan had been back home where he belonged for a whole four days already. But believe me, if my mother and sister ever caught him sneezing, he'd be bunking with me tonight again. Guaranteed.

"I won't catch cold," said Jonathan from the driveway. "I'm swimming standing up."

"Well, stop swimming and come in here and play cards or you're out of the game."

Jonathan ran back inside the garage and shook the water from his hair. He straddled my old tricycle and picked up his cards from the table. He looked at his hand, then at Goog. His hand. Goog. His hand. Goog.

Goog moaned. "Hurry up, Jonathan."

"Got any eights?"

Goog handed over two cards and shook his head. "I don't know how you do it."

"Thanks. Elliot taught me everything I know," Jonathan said, wiping his face with his T-shirt. Goog looked over to me and I shook my head. What a kid.

Goog threw his cards down on the table. "I wish I played ball as good as you play cards. That last game we played, I stunk."

I didn't argue with him. There are times when even a best friend stretching the truth for you won't help. Goog hadn't really stunk. But he was close. In the second inning he struck out with a man on third. He made an error in the fourth that cost two runs. And then he hit into an inning-ending double play in the fifth.

"You got that good hit in the fifth inning," I said. "And you scored from second when Billy got that hit."

Goog sighed. "But by then they were five runs ahead of us."

Yeah. It was a pretty lame game, all right. And to think I had to watch it sitting next to Corinne

Morrisey. Yech. That was even worse than watching the team lose to the Giants.

"You'll get them next time," I said.

"That's right. Just wait until next time," Jonathan said. "Next time Corinne will be on the team, right, Goog?"

"Says who?" I said.

"Says Goog," said Jonathan. "That's what you told me, isn't it, Goog?"

Goog shrugged. "Well, she said that she wants to be on the team."

"I know she says she *wants* to be on our team. She told Jonathan. She told me. She told practically everybody that she wants to be on the team. That doesn't mean she *will* be on the team."

"Well, I'm just telling you what she asked the coach. She told him she wants to be shortstop."

"But I'm the shortstop. That's my position."

"Yeah. That's Elliot's position," chimed in Jonathan.

"Of course it's your position. You're our shortstop," said Goog. "Besides, Mr. Anderson didn't say she was on the team. Not definitely . . . yet."

"Not definitely . . . yet? What does that mean?"

"Nothing. Nothing. He's just sort of working on it . . . or something. But I don't think you have to worry about Corinne taking your place."

"I'm not worried about her taking my place," I said, shuffling my hand. "Take my place! . . . That's a hot one."

"Well, she did take your place on the swim team, Elliot . . . and she's doing a pretty good job there, too."

I stared at Goog.

"Well, anyway . . . she can catch. I played catch with her a few times and—"

"You what?"

"Played catch."

"You're kidding."

"It was just a few times. In my backyard. Don't worry about her," said Goog.

"Who's worried? Me? Worried about Corinne Morrisey? Ha!"

"I mean, even if she does play on our team and does get to play shortstop, you know how to play lots of positions, Elliot. Third base. Center field. You can even pitch, right? . . . Elliot? I said, you can even pitch, right?"

I stared at Goog. This girl was drilling worm holes in his brain.

Goog picked up his cards from the table. He shuffled his hand. "Are we still playing this game? . . . Any fives?" I handed over two cards. "I don't know why you don't like her," Goog said, straightening his hand.

"What's to like?" I muttered.

"Goog says she dives good and swims good," started Jonathan. "She plays basketball and soccer. She can catch and hit and skateboard, she plays the piano, she—"

"Okay. Okay. We get the picture."

I didn't care what they said. Nobody was that good at everything. It wasn't human . . . which she probably wasn't. That toe of mine doesn't tingle for nothing. There had to be something she couldn't do. Something she didn't know. She's got to trip up sometime, and when she does, the old Wonder Worm will be right there to catch her. NOT. Ha.

The only thing was, I hadn't really come up with a plan yet. The wormy side of my brain hadn't been used for so long, it was taking a while for me to jump-start it. But something had to come to me. It had to.

Beep. Beep.

Jeffrey's Jeep pulled into the driveway and stopped. Jeff hopped out and waved as he jogged into the garage.

"Hi, you guys. What's up?"

"Nothing," I said, dropping my cards. "Absolutely nothing."

Jeff picked up Jonathan and flipped him over his shoulder.

"Goog and Elliot are talking about girls." Jonathan giggled while hanging upside down.

"Girls?" said Jeff, placing Jonathan back down. I sneezed again. "You getting a cold?" he asked as Jonathan gave me another one of his blessings.

"Peat moss." I nodded at the bag and sneezed once more.

"It's the peat moss, or he's allergic to Corinne Morrisey," Goog said with a hoot.

"The swimmer? The girl who can do the 100 meter faster than you?"

"She plays shortstop, too," said Jonathan.

"She doesn't play shortstop!" I said with a sneeze. "Not yet anyway."

"Yup. He is allergic to her," said Goog, laughing.

"Who wouldn't be allergic to her? She's worse than poison ivy, I tell you."

Jeff straddled the little trike, his knees almost reaching his chin. He gathered the cards on our table, straightened out the few stray ones sticking out from the pile, and started shuffling the deck.

"Some girls can get under your skin, all right," he said, looking over to me. "Just between us guys," he said as he shuffled, "it's a weird thing about girls. . . ." He didn't have to tell me that. "One day you think they're the worst, and the next day you begin thinking, 'Hey, they're not too bad.'" He was right. That was weird. Totally weird. Unbelievably weird. "It happens," he said.

"When did it happen to you?" Goog asked.

My brother shook his head. "I don't remember exactly. . . . It just sort of snuck up on me. Dad told me the same thing happened to him."

"Just snuck up on you? Wow," said Goog.

"Wow," echoed Jonathan.

Wow? What loonies.

"Jeff, do you think it could be sneaking up on me

right now?" asked Goog.

"Could be," Jeff said. "And other things change, too."

"Like what?" asked Goog, leaning closer.

"Yeah, like what?" asked Jonathan, leaning in close like Goog.

Jeffrey kept shuffling the cards. "Like, one day you don't want to take a bath. . . . next day you're taking five of them."

"Get out of here!" said Goog.

Jeff nodded. "Even a shower! You're wearing your underwear three days straight, all of a sudden you're thinking about not just changing them . . . but what color they are."

I stared at my brother. My big brother. The brother who knew everything there was to know about anything. He looked okay, but I think he was spending too many hours at that pool. He was sounding like his brain was waterlogged.

"Who knows, Elliot," Jeff said. "Maybe one day you'll even be glad you're an uncle."

"Yeah," chimed in the Squirt as he kicked a deflated soccer ball.

That was it. This was getting too weird. I was out of there.

Beep. Beep beep. Beep.

The old Volvo pulled into the driveway behind the Jeep. Before she even got out of the car, we could hear Grace complaining about Jeffrey's car being in her way, the rain, her frizzy hair, wet feet, the puddles. . . . I decided to stay in the garage. It was safer than being in her path, even with my brother's weird talk.

Grace walked around the big puddle and stood at the foot of the garage just under the overhang and out of the rain. Her glasses were spotted with raindrops and the grocery bag she shifted to her other arm was wet and limp. "What are all of you doing in here?"

Jonathan jumped off of the old scooter and ran over to Grace, waving his arms. "Out. Out," he shouted.

"Jonathan," she said. "That isn't very polite. What's gotten into you?"

"Out. You have to leave, Auntie Grace. You have to. We're talking guy talk, and you're not a guy. You're a girl."

"Jonathan!"

"You have to leave," he insisted. "Go. Guys only.

Right, Elliot?"

"Right!"

"Right," said Jeff and Goog.

"You're all incorrigible."

I didn't know what that word meant exactly, but I was betting it was something I would be glad to be called.

"I'm telling Mother that all of you are a bad influence on Jonathan." Grace looked at us and made her usual big sister dopey face, then turned and walked away in one of her huffs. We could still hear her huffing and puffing all the way up the back deck until the screen door opened and banged shut.

"Way to go, Jonathan!" I shouted as we all high-fived him.

The Squirt was getting to be okay.

10

THE SECRET WEAPON

OH, NO. ITCH EMERGENCY! I was getting another one of those million scillion antsy itches under my cast. I did a quick belly-worm crawl under my bed. Where was that stick I'd rolled under here? I pushed aside my sneaker with the hole in the toe and blew away a giant dust ball. (I guess Mom was right about vacuuming under the bed.) I nudged a stack of books. Uh-oh. So that's where that lost library book from last year was. . . .

"Ooh . . . eeh." The itch was getting worse. I coughed, and almost sucked down another dust ball. Where are you, stick? . . . Ah, there it was. Up against the wall. I stretched out my good arm and wiggled my fingers.

"Gotcha."

I scrunched out from under the bed, leaned against the footboard, and let the stick do its job.

"Aaaaaaahhhhh."

Dumb itch. Dumb broken arm. I looked at my cast.

GO, ALCORN . . . BRING US LUCK, ELLIOT . . . TO THE BEST SHORTSTOP . . . NEED YOU . . . Looking at what the guys had written was the only good part about having this broken arm. Even though I couldn't play for the rest of the season, they had still made me feel part of the team.

I sighed and stared up at the calendar tacked on the closet door. No matter how many times I counted the days, I still had two more weeks to go before Dr. Margolis took off the cast. Just two more weeks. The problem was Little League play-offs were in just one week. Dr. Margolis would never take my cast off before then. Even if I begged. . . . But . . . I wondered if he would if the whole team begged. He might. He could. . . . If Doc only knew how much the guys needed me. If he only knew they might not win without me.

Two weeks. I patted the green monster and flopped on the bed. No. Doctor Margolis wasn't going to take it off before then no matter who asked him. I'd probably be too rusty to help the guys out anyway.

What a summer. No swimming. No baseball. And then, of course, to top it all, there was Corinne. Of all the neighborhoods in all the towns, she had to move next to Goog. Worse, I think Goog liked it. He was with her practically every day. Eesh. I didn't know how he stood it. My brain still hadn't come up with any wormy ideas for her, either. Not one rotten, humiliating, torturing idea. I was really beginning to worry that my Wonder Worm days were over.

About the only thing good about any of this was that I was pretty sure nothing else could go wrong before the summer was over. Yesterday my mother almost got me to change little Ellie's diaper. After being that close to baby poop, what else could happen?

"Elliot? Elliot, are you up there?"

"Uh-huh," I called back as I doodled on my doodle wall next to my bed.

"Caroline is here with Jonathan and little Ellie."

"Uh-huh."

"We're going for a walk."

"Uh-huh."

"Do you want to come with us?"

"Uh-uh."

"Come with us, Elliot," Jonathan called out, pounding up the stairs. "Come with us," he said over and over as he tramped down the hallway and into my room. "Come, Elliot. Grammie and my mom say we can have some ice cream after we walk little Ellie."

I stopped doodling and dropped the marker to the floor. "Naah."

"Why? What's the matter?"

"Nothing."

"You look like something's the matter."

"Nothing's the matter," I said.

"You sort of look the way you looked when you ate too much and your stomach hurt. Remember that time? When you and Goog ate too much?"

"I remember."

"Does your stomach hurt like that again?"

"No, my stomach doesn't hurt again. Nothing hurts, Jonathan. I'm fine."

"Then how come you don't want to eat ice cream?"

I looked at the names on my cast. " I guess I could eat some ice cream. Okay, I'll come with you. Nothing else to do around here anyway."

Jonathan took hold of my hand and yanked me off the bed. "We're going to take little Ellie to Johnson Park."

"Johnson Park?" We walked out of the bedroom. "You know what? . . . I think that's where Goog and the rest of the team are practicing tonight. Come on, Squirt. If we hurry, maybe we can still watch them play," I said, skipping down the stairs two at a time.

Hurry was not a word my mother or sister knew when it came to little Ellie. It took us longer to strap and unstrap Elyse in her car seat, and lug her carriage and the rest of her baby junk in and out of the car, than it took us to drive to the park.

Caroline propped up Ellie in the carriage and Mom covered her up with a blanket and tied a dopey-looking cap on her head.

"Isn't she going to sweat with all that stuff piled on top of her?" I asked. "It's eighty-five degrees."

"She's a baby, Elliot," my sister said as Ellie squirmed. "And besides, this is just a light little baby blanket, for heaven's sake."

A blanket is a blanket in my book. Especially when it's eighty-five degrees. Jonathan looked at me and shook his head. Yeah. The squirtlette didn't have a chance. My mother and Caroline had started to push the carriage toward the first turn around the lake when, luckily, I saw the guys on the baseball field.

"Can I go watch practice now, Mom?"

She made one of her grammie goos at Ellie and nodded to me without really looking. "Just for a little while," she said. "We'll send Jonathan for you when we're ready to leave, and then we'll all have some ice cream."

I heard Jonathan say he wanted chocolate with vanilla marshmallow goop just as I hurdled a park bench and ran toward the field.

"Goog! Guys! Zack, Mikey, hi!" I shouted from behind the fence by the visitors' dugout. Mikey whiffed at a pitch Zack had just thrown and the ball rattled around the chain links of the batter's cage. Goog threw a ball to Billy Zakian, who was standing on first base, and waved to me with his glove. I waved back as he and Billy ran over to the fence.

"Elliot, are we glad to see you!" Billy said.

I knew it. I knew they needed me for the play-offs. Rusty or not. That did it. I was going to have Mom call Dr. Margolis first thing tomorrow morning.

"Listen, guys," I started, "I've been thinking. Tomorrow I'm going to—"

"First let us tell you about practice," interrupted Goog.

"Oh, right. How's it going?" I figured I'd wait to tell them about my great idea.

"Un-be-liev-ably . . . great!" said Goog.

Wait. Whoa. Did the Goog say "great?"

"Elliot, we are going to crush the Giants. I mean, cr-ush them."

"We are? I mean, you are?"

Billy smiled. "Elliot, we're saved."

"Saved?"

"You'll never believe it. Guess who's playing on our team? You'll never guess in a million years."

Toe-tingle alert. Toe-tingle alert.

I don't know why I even asked it. "Who?"

"Who else?" Goog said. "Corinne. Corinne Morrisey."

Goog was excited. I could tell. I had known him long enough to recognize all the signs. His eyes were bugging out and his voice was high and squeaky. He was talking a mile a minute, sputtering spit all over the place.

". . . and because you broke your arm and couldn't play, which of course you know, anyway, we were short one man, I mean, one person, and Corinne wanted to play—Mr. Anderson checked the rules-and-regulations stuff—and what do you know, Corinne's on our team. Just like that!"

"What do you know. Just like that," I said, wiping Goog's spit off of Sluggo the arm.

"And can she hit!" said Billy, who was acting almost as excited as Goog.

Goog stuffed a wad of gum into his mouth. "Rockets."

Rockets. Oh, boy.

"She'll smash Joey Capelletti's curve ball right over the fence."

"You know it, Billy," Goog said as they both laughed and gave each other a high five.

Billy leaned closer to me. "And she's a girl," he

whispered. "Can you believe it, Elliot? A girl."

I believed it, all right.

"Come on and watch her," said Billy. "Goog, go show Elliot your double-play combination."

"Double play?" I asked.

Goog sucked in a bubble. "She does it almost as good as we used to, El."

I followed him over to the bench. Yup. There she was on the field. Playing shortstop.

"Elliot! Hey, Elliot!" shouted Nick from first base. "Wait till Joey C. gets a load of our secret weapon, huh?"

The "secret weapon" looked over and waved to me. I think my arm waved back. It must have done that on its own, because I didn't tell it do anything that stupid. I watched Corinne make double play after double play. Catch pop-ups. Gun the ball over to first. It was my worst nightmare coming true. She was probably going to be wearing my number, too. The war was over before it ever got started. The old Wonder Worm was squished. Squashed. Going, going, gone.

"Elliot?" Jonathan was tugging my T-shirt from

behind. "Grammie and Mommy say it's time to get ice cream," he said. I kept watching Corinne. "Elliot? Is that—"

"Yup. It's her." Now she was doing turns and pivots.

"Is she the shortstop?"

"She's the shortstop."

"She's on your team?"

"She's on . . . my team." I stared down at my cast. No rush getting this off now.

Jonathan patted my shoulder. "Don't worry about her, Elliot. She'll never be as good as you are."

I looked at him. He smiled back. "Hey, Squirt," I said. "Let's go get some ice cream."

"Right now?"

"Right now."

"Chocolate with vanilla marshmallow, remember?"

"Chocolate with vanilla marshmallow," I said, hopping off the bench.

"Hey, Elliot," Jonathan said as we walked away from the field. "How about a game of Candyland when we get home?"

"How about two?"

11

BOO

"EL-LI-OT . . . EL-LI-OT . . . EL-LI-OT."

The crowd was cheering. Feet started stamping.

Bottom of the ninth. Two on. Two out. We were down by one run. The pennant was on the line.

"EL-LI-OT . . . EL-LI-OT."

Goog stepped out of the dugout. He squinted into the lights as he searched the stands. Then he saw me. He waved.

"They need you, son," Dad said, patting my back.

"But, your arm, Elliot," Mom said in a worried voice. "Your arm is still in a cast."

"My team needs me, Mom. I have to go."

"You're so brave. I'm so proud of you, Elliot."

"Elliot! Elliot! Wait!" Peggy said, running up the bleachers with my jersey. "Here's your uniform." She

handed it to me and smiled. "I brought it with me, just in case."

"Thanks."

Lucky number 7. I pulled the jersey over my head.

"EL . . . LI . . . OT . . . EL . . . LI . . . OT."

I made my way through the cheering crowd down the bleacher steps, then jumped the rail into the dugout. The team huddled around me.

"Do we need you," Zack Wilson sighed, wiping his brow.

"Do we ever," said Mikey Gries.

"The team isn't the same without you," said Danny Jacobus.

I looked around the dugout. "But, what about Corinne?"

"She choked," said Goog.

"Double choked," said Billy. "She's already struck out two times. She couldn't hit Joey's curve with a bat as wide as a tree trunk."

"Can you do it, Elliot?" asked Zack. "Can you save the game for us? . . . Can you do it, Elliot?"

I looked up at the crowd in the bleachers. I looked around the dugout at the guys. "Where's my bat?"

"EL-LI-OT . . . EL-LI-OT."

I climbed out of the dugout and took three swings in the on-deck circle. I walked up to the batter's box. Joey stared at me from the pitcher's mound. I dug my heels into the dirt around home plate. I stared back. The umpire flipped down his mask.

"Play ball!" he yelled.

Joey went into his windup.

"EL-LI-OT . . . EL-LI-OT."

A big fat fastball was hurling right toward the sweet part of my bat. One good swing and it was bye, bye, baby.

"EL-LI-OT . . . EL-LI-OT."

"Elliot? . . . Elliot?"

"Huh?"

Peggy yanked my hand and pulled me off the kitchen chair. "What are you doing, daydreaming or something? Come on. We're all waiting for you. You don't want to be late for the game, do you?"

"Elliot? Where were you?" my mother said from the front seat as I opened the car door and climbed in behind her. "Didn't you hear me calling you?"

"Yes . . . I mean, no . . . I mean, never mind." I pulled the seat-belt strap over my shoulder. "Ooh. Dad. Remember, we have to pick up Jonathan."

Peggy stared at me as my father turned on the ignition and backed the station wagon out of the driveway. "What's the reason you're so concerned about Jonathan?"

"No reason."

"Right. What are you up to, you little weasel?"

"Peggy, don't call your brother a weasel," Mom said, turning around to look at both of us. I grinned at my sister. "But what are you up to, Elliot?"

"I'm not up to anything. Geez . . ." My father turned the corner, and Peggy rolled down the window on her side. I grinned one of those wormy grins that took every one of my nine and a half years to perfect. Yes! I was ba-ack. It had taken a while, but the old Wonder Worm brain finally came through. I had the perfect plan all worked out for you-know-who. It was devious. It was sneaky. It was . . . me. And the Squirt was going to be my little wormy helper. How could my parents get mad at me when the Squirt was part of the action? I ask you, how perfect was that?

The car pulled up to Caroline and Peter's house, and Jonathan came running down the walk. My sister waved from the front porch as Jonathan climbed into the backseat next to me.

"Assistant Jonathan reporting, Chief," he said with a salute.

"What's he talking about? Assistant what, Elliot?" Peggy asked as the breeze whipped a piece of her hair into her mouth.

"Just my assistant," I said.

"Jon-a-than. Tell me. Right now."

"He's just my assistant," I said before the Squirt could answer.

"Right, Elliot. Assistant what?"

"Yes, Elliot. Assistant what?" my mother asked. Sisters. Now she had to get my mother all interested and nosy.

"Nothing . . ." I said as my mother kept staring. "Nothing."

"Yeah. It's nothing, Grammie. I'm just going to help Elliot boo, that's all."

"Boo?" said my sister.

"Boo?" said my mother.

"Boo?" said my father.

"Oh, it's no big deal," I said. "We're just going to boo the Giants a little bit."

"Yeah. Just the Giants," said Jonathan. "And Corinne Morrisey. Don't forget her, right, Elliot?"

"Elliot," my mother said. "That is not nice."

"I know. That's why I'm doing it."

"Elliot."

"Elliot."

"I'm kidding! . . . Mom, Dad, I'm kidding!"

"You better be," said Dad, giving me the eye from the rearview mirror. "You are not going to see your team play to boo anyone."

"I said I was kidding. . . . I am." (Not.)

We got to the ball field in plenty of time before the game started and still almost didn't find seats. The place was packed. Mostly because Giants rooters were hogging the stands. Joey Capelletti must have had everybody he was related to sitting in the bleachers. JOEY banners took up two whole rows. The five of us climbed up to the fourth row, and Mr. and Mrs. Ackerman slid over on the bench so we could sit down.

My mother waved to Goog's mom and dad, who were sitting down in front. "Elliot, are those people sitting there the Gugliocello's new neighbors?"

"Uh-huh."

"Evelyn said that they were very nice."

Nice. How nice could they be? They'd created Corinne, hadn't they?

"Look, Elliot," Jonathan shouted as he tugged my good arm. "There's Goog. Hi, Goog!"

"Mom, I'll be back in a minute," I said. "Goog is waving me down to the dugout."

"Me, too. He's waving at me, too," said Jonathan. "That means I can come with you, right, Elliot?"

"Yeah, you can come with me," I answered as he followed me down the bleachers. The Squirt was safer with me than up there in the stands. I didn't want to take any chances of ruining the Big Plan.

"Elliot! Jonathan!" Goog shouted as he helped me hoist Jonathan over the rail. "Look, guys. Elliot's here."

"Alcorn!" Nick Locastro called out. "Ellie!" shouted Kevin and Zack at the same time.

"Thumb noogies," yelled Billy. "More thumb noogies."

"Thumb noogies for me, too," said Jonathan right before we all started to elbow bash one another. "I want to do the team handshake, too."

"Come here, Jonathan." Corinne walked over and smiled. "I'll do the handshake with you."

Jonathan looked at Corinne and then at me. He stood on his toes and whispered up to me, "Should I, Elliot?"

I looked at Corinne standing there in her uniform. She would pick *one* as her number.

"Elliot, should I do the handshake with her?" Jonathan whispered again.

"If she knows the team handshake . . . go ahead."

"Reds, Reds, the other guys are dead!" Corinne chanted as she gave Jonathan two thumb noogies and an elbow bash.

"She knew it, Elliot," Jonathan said, turning back to me as Corinne grinned.

I wouldn't have expected anything else.

Corinne took off her cap and shook her hair loose. "The colored trim goes with my hair," she said.

Goes with her hair? . . . And she calls herself a short-stop. All of a sudden I couldn't wait for the game to begin. Mr. Anderson walked out to home plate with the batting order, and I called Jonathan to leave and head up to our battle station.

"One more noogie for good luck," said Goog as the rest of the guys huddled around me. "Wish you were with us," Goog said, patting my back. I gave him another elbow bash, this time with my good arm.

"Have a good one, guys," I called out as I helped Jonathan over the rail. "Good luck, everybody."

"Thanks, Elliot," Nick and Zack called back.

"Thanks, Elliot," said Corinne.

I walked up the bleacher steps with Jonathan and laughed to myself. Me, say good luck to her? Was she kidding? What a macaroni.

"Go, Reds!" I shouted, and clapped as the team took the field. "Go, Goog!"

"There's Corinne," Jonathan said as he sat between my mother and me. "Should I do it now, Elliot?"

My mother looked over and gave me one of her official Mom looks.

"He's kidding, Mom. I told you in the car. . . . All that booing business . . . I was kidding." I looked at Jonathan. "No booing, Squirt. Don't you know that isn't nice?"

"But I thought I was your assistant," he whispered.

My mother still had the Mom look.

"Just watch the game, Jonathan."

This was going to be a delicate manuever. A very delicate manuever.

Billy Zakian was on the mound for our team and got the Giants out in the first inning, one, two, three. But Joey struck out our first three batters, so the inning ended with the score 0–0. It was all goose eggs until the top of the sixth inning, when all of a sudden the Giants got two squibbly little hits and had runners on first and second with only one out. The Giants' third baseman hit a double off Billy, and before the inning ended, we were down by two runs.

"Come on, Goog," I yelled as Goog stepped up to the plate in the bottom of the seventh with two men already out. "You can do it. Come on, Goog!"

Joey kicked the dirt on the pitcher's mound and

stood on the rubber. He stared hard at Goog. He kept shaking his head at the catcher.

"He's coming in with the curve, Goog. Get ready for it. Look curve all the way," I said to myself as the crowd started chanting, "We want a hit!"

Joey threw one of his wicked curves all right, but the old Goog was waiting for it, and *POW!* he smacked it right through the legs of the second baseman.

"That a way, Goog!" I shouted as he rounded first base. The right fielder bobbled the ball and Goog kept running right to second.

"Go, Goog!" yelled Jonathan.

"Slide, Goog! Slide!" I screamed as the ball got to second just about the same time as he did.

"Safe!" the umpire shouted.

Jonathan and I jumped up and down. "Did you see that?" I shouted. "He was flying."

"Flying!" shouted Jonathan. "Nobody runs like the Goog, right, Elliot?"

We were slapping each other on the back as Nicky Locastro came up to the plate. "Get a hit, Nick. Get a hit, Nick," the crowd started chanting. Joey threw the first pitch. Nicky swung.

"Strike one!" yelled the umpire.

"Wait for a good one," I shouted through cupped hands. "Look 'em over."

"Look 'em over," repeated Jonathan.

Joey went into his windup. He threw it toward the plate.

"Strike two!"

"We want a hit! We want a hit!"

Foul ball.

"We want a hit! We want a hit!"

Nicky barely tapped the ball and it rolled down the third base line.

"A perfect bunt!" my father shouted, getting to his feet.

"Holy Cow! The little knucklehead actually bunted! With two strikes. And it worked! It worked!"

The crowd was going wild. Everyone was standing up, stamping their feet. Even my mother was stamping, and I don't think she even knew why. We had runners on first and third, two out, and the go-ahead run was coming up to the plate.

"Who's up now?" Jonathan asked as he stood on his seat, trying to see over the people in front of him.

"Who's up, Elliot?"

I sat down. I didn't know if I wanted to see any more. It was Corinne.

"Strike one!" yelled the umpire.

I stood up. Corinne backed away from home plate. She took a couple of practice swings, then got back into the batter's box.

"Is it time to boo yet?" Jonathan asked me.

"Not yet," I whispered back.

Joey went into his windup.

"Strike two!"

"Now?" asked Jonathan.

"Soon." I smiled. This was too good to be true. She was choking. Runners in scoring position, and she was choking. Game on the line and she was choking. This was perfect. This was even better than I had imagined.

"Ball one."

Goog yelled to her from third. "Come on, Corinne. You can do it."

Nicky shouted from first. "Let's go, Corinne." The rest of the team was off the bench, all standing at the edge of the dugout, yelling encouragement, too.

"Foul ball!" shouted the umpire as she hit a weak dribbler behind home plate.

If she struck out now and ended the game, the Giants were going to win. The Giants were going to win easy, and we were going to be shut out. We were going to lose. Big time.

"Ball two."

I looked down at my cast. I stared at Billy's name, and the Goog's, Zack's, Mikey's, Kevin's. My friends. My team.

My team.

Joey was staring down Corinne. Corinne was staring down Joey.

I stood up. Forget being a worm. "Go, Corinne!" I shouted. "We want a hit! We want a hit!"

Jonathan looked at me. "I thought you didn't want her to get a hit, Elliot. I thought you wanted to be the shortstop."

"Shortstop? Aaahh, anybody can play shortstop, Squirt . . . but you have to have a real arm to play third. . . . Come on, Corinne! We want a hit! We want a hit!"

"We really want a hit, Elliot?" asked Jonathan.

"We really want a hit," I said.

Joey went into his windup.

"We want a hit!" Jonathan and I yelled together.
"We want a hit!"

SMACK!

12

THE GODFATHER

"OKAY, ELLIOT . . . LET'S HAVE another one. Smile!"

I looked at my father and grinned as he snapped the picture.

"Let's have one more," my mother said. "Come on, my two Ellies, just one more."

"Mom," I said through another grin, "my cheeks are beginning to hurt from all this smiling."

All of our relatives packed into Caroline and Peter's living room started to laugh, and then applauded as the cameras finally stopped clicking for a while.

"She's squirming a little," I said to Caroline as she lifted the baby from my arms. "She's probably sick of all these dumb pictures, too."

"Just like her uncle." My sister laughed, patting Ellie's back.

I got up from the chair and squeezed in between and around aunts, uncles, and cousins, trying to make my way to the dining room. Food. I needed food. I just hoped there was some left after this crowd got to it. Our whole family said my cousin George could inhale a cow.

"I was very proud of you today in church, Elliot," Aunt Margaret said before I could reach the buffet table. "You did a fine job."

I had done a pretty good job of being a godfather, if I do say so myself. I answered when the priest told me to answer, and I didn't drop Ellie when it was my turn to hold her. Even when my arm started itching. Little Ellie was the real champ, though. She hardly even cried, and considering that goofy lacy getup they dressed her in, that was something. She cried when the priest poured the water over her head, but hey, who wants water dribbling all over you? Yeah, she did okay.

"Thanks, Aunt Margaret," I said as she hugged me. I tried to breathe.

Aunt Margaret was sort of big. When I was Jonathan's age, I thought she was hiding pillows under her blouse. She felt as soft as pillows anyway. She still did. "Uh, thanks again, Aunt Margaret," I said, taking a deep breath as she finally let go. "I'm going to get something to eat now."

"Elliot, you did an excellent job today at the christening," said Aunt Katie. "A very fine job."

"Thanks, Aunt Katie. Excuse me, but I'm just going to go into the dining room and get some food and—"

"Congratulations, Godfather," Uncle Hank said as he patted me on the back.

"Thanks. Thanks, Uncle Hank. I'm just going to get something to—"

"Elliot! Elliot! There you are," Grace said. "Come on over here with me." She yanked my hand before I even got a toe into the dining room.

"But I haven't eaten yet," I said.

"Oh, is that all you ever think about? Eating?"

"It is when I haven't eaten."

"Come on. Peter wants another picture of you and me and Ellie. You know, Godmother, Godfather, and Ellie, and Grandpop wants one with all of you weird

Alcorn Toe people. Something about four generations of sideways toes, I don't know."

She dragged me onto the screened porch and Peter positioned us by some wilted plants. Caroline handed over Ellie to Grace. Ellie squirmed. She didn't like Grace either. The kid was going to be all right.

"Smile, everybody," Peter said as we stared at the camera. "Great shot."

I blinked back the spots as Grandpop then manuevered Uncle Jack and Aunt Clara around Ellie and me for the family toe picture. After a few snapshots, Grandpop insisted we all take our shoes and socks off for a real toe shot. Grandma said he was crazy, but we did it. Dad even videoed the whole thing. He did a zooming close-up of Ellie's teenie, tiny one.

Ellie finally started to wail and saved us from any more pictures. At least for a while. "Oooh," Caroline said, taking her from Grace's arms, "she's starving."

No kidding. Me, too. I worked up an appetite being a godfather. I can imagine what Ellie worked up being the baby. I finally made it to the table, grabbed a sandwich, and piled my plate with whatever other food I could stab, spoon, and spear.

"Excuse me. Excuse me," I said as my plate and I tried to make our way through a maze of relatives. We weren't making too much progress. Every two feet one of my aunts or uncles was either kissing or congratulating me or asking how my arm was. The only place to go was up, so I started climbing steps and ended up at the top of the stairs.

Peace. Quiet. And food. I was just about to shovel in some potato salad when I heard a bedroom door creak behind me. I turned around. There was Jonathan.

"Hey, there you are," I said. "What are you doing in there all by yourself?"

"Nothing."

I bit into the sandwich. "Nothing?" I said as a glop of mayonnaise fell from my chin. "What are you doing in your room doing nothing?"

Jonathan sat down on the top step next to me. "I don't know. Just felt like it. I was just sitting on my bed."

I bit into a dill pickle. The juice ran down my fingers. "How come you're not downstairs with your sister?" I asked, slurping my thumb.

Jonathan shrugged. He was quiet. He didn't look at me.

"Yeah. It's pretty crowded down there," I said. "Did you get smothered by Aunt Margaret?"

Jonathan shook his head.

"Well, just make sure you take a deep breath before she hugs you." I took another bite of the sandwich. "Did you eat?" He shook his head again. "How come?"

"Don't feel like it." Jonathan stared down at his shoes. He was chewing on his bottom lip.

"Guess you didn't get too much sleep last night, huh? . . . I bet Ellie was probably crying all the time, right? . . . Babies. Yeah, that's what babies do. . . . Cry . . . keep you awake . . . always wanting somebody to hold them."

Jonathan kept staring down at his shoes. "Mom's always holding her. Daddy, too."

I nodded. "That's babies for you. They always want to be held or fed or rocked. Totally inconsiderate. Like they're the only ones that are important, right?"

Jonathan looked at me. "Right. Right."

"But, hey, you're the big brother."

"So?"

"So? So, you have to show her the ropes."

"I do?"

"Sure. You have to train her."

"Train her?" said Jonathan. "Like Uncle Hank had to train his dog?"

"Hmm . . . sort of. But dogs are easier."

"How do I train my sister, Elliot?"

I took another bite of the sandwich. "Well, first," I said as I chewed, "first, you have to have a plan."

Jonathan frowned. "I don't have a plan."

I swallowed. "You make one."

"I don't know how."

I smiled. "No problem. I'm great at plans. I'll help you. It's sort of a big-brother tradition. Jeffrey showed Grace, Peggy, and me, and now you'll show Elyse."

"But who will show me?"

"You? Me, of course!"

"You will, Elliot?"

"Sure. We'll have your sister trained in no time."

"You mean, show her the ropes?"

"You got it."

Jonathan smiled. "Elliot?"

"Yeah, Squirt?"

"Can I have a bite of your sandwich? I'm hungry."

13

ARMED AND DANGEROUS

"My arm looks so weird, Dad."

"That's just because of the cast. Remember, you had it on for over six weeks," my father said as we drove home from the doctor's office.

"It looks so . . . yechy . . . so white and wrinkled or something. It doesn't even look like my other one."

"You'll be fine, son. A few days playing outside in the sunshine, shagging flies with Goog, and your arm will look just like it always looked."

We turned down Elm Street. "Goog left for a week's vacation yesterday," I said. "Nick and Billy, too. There's nobody around to play catch with."

"Well, then," my father said over the ticking blinker as we turned on our street, "maybe this afternoon you, your brother, and I can go to the driving range and hit a few buckets of balls. What do you say to that?"

"Could we? Great. I'm probably real rusty. I could use the practice."

"So can I," my father said, laughing.

We pulled into the driveway. My mother was standing by the front door and waving. I got out of the car and waved back with my two good arms as I ran across the lawn and up the front porch steps.

"So? What did Dr. Margolis say?" Mom asked while holding the door open for us.

"He's fine. As good as new," Dad said, picking up the newspaper on the hall table before going into the living room.

"But it looks weird," I said, lifting my arm up to my mother's face.

"Oh, it looks all right." She gave me a kiss. "You are a very, very lucky boy, Elliot Alcorn. Now don't you even think about diving off that back deck or anyone else's again. Do you hear me?"

"Absolutely," I said following her through the dining room and into the kitchen. I couldn't even remember why I'd done it in the first place.

"Where's Jeff?" I asked, sitting down at the table.

"Oh, he's around somewhere," Mom said as she walked over to the counter and untwisted the tie on the plastic wrap of a loaf of bread.

She opened the refrigerator door and took out a jar of mustard and a stack of paper-wrapped lunch meat. She pulled the tape from the wrapper. I smelled Swiss cheese.

"He can't be too far off. He knows I was about to make sandwiches for lunch. Why do you want Jeff?"

I flexed my arm. My muscle had disappeared, too. "I was just going to ask him if he wanted to go with Dad and me this afternoon and hit some golf balls."

"This afternoon?" Mom turned. "Oh, Honey, Jeffrey can't go today."

"He can't?"

"And neither can your father. As a matter of fact, neither can you."

"How come? Where are we going?"

My mother turned back to the counter and spread mustard on a piece of bread. "Well, Dad and Jeff have to go over to Aunt Katie's house and fix her screened porch. She said the mosquitoes are eating her alive and she doesn't think she can last another day."

"What about me?" I asked, walking over to her and reaching for a piece of cheese. "Where do I have to go?"

"Nowhere." She looked at me and smiled. "Caroline and Peter are going to a wedding, and I want you to stay here with me and help with Jonathan and little Ellie. Caroline asked if we'd baby-sit."

"We? She didn't ask me!"

Mom laughed. "Oh, Elliot," she said, "you know what I mean."

Did I ever. Now besides Jonathan, I had the little weezer to worry about. Not only did she pee all the time, but she was pooping her brains out, too. Let me tell you, baby poop smells as bad as any other poop.

"But, Mom, I just got my cast off. I wanted to do good stuff."

"I need you, Elliot. Besides, Jonathan likes being with you. And you love little Ellie. You love them both."

I made a face.

"You don't fool me, Elliot Alcorn."

She kissed me again. I can't argue with my mother when she kisses me.

I sat down in the rocking chair and my mother handed me the baby. She didn't even have to tell me to hold Elyse's head. I was getting pretty good at knowing how to hold her.

"Here's the bottle," Jonathan said, handing it to me.

The pip-squeak opened her little mouth and started to chow down. What an appetite! She could chug down a whole bottle in nothing flat. Pretty soon she was going to be piling on the pounds, that was for sure. I think she even felt a little heavier already. Her legs were starting to get little rolls of fat. Sort of like Peggy in a bathing suit. And her face wasn't so scrunched anymore either. I guess she was getting sort of cute . . . for a pip-squeak.

"She's hungry, huh, Elliot?" Jonathan said as he knelt in front of me.

I watched her suck the life out of the nipple. "Yup. She's a little pig, all right." Jonathan and I laughed as I tried to pry the bottle from her mouth.

"She's squirming, Mom," I said as Elyse started to kick.

"She needs to be burped."

Goog should have been here. He knew all about burping.

"Let me lift her for you," Mom said as she repositioned the baby on my shoulder.

"What do I do now?"

"You pat her back, Elliot. . . . Lightly . . . that's it."

I kept patting her, and then before I knew it, we all heard this sound like an alien was in her stomach and . . . *whoop!* "Yuck! What was that?" I said not able to move.

"She burped," Mom said, taking the baby from me.

"What else?" I smelled something disgusting.

"Oh, she just spit up a little."

"A little?" I said, looking at my shoulder. "Gross."

Jonathan laughed. "I think she slimed you."

"Wait until she slimes you, Squirt," I said, rushing out of the room and into the kitchen to wipe off the glop.

"Elliot?" my mother called from the other room.

"I'm not changing any stinky diapers," I yelled back.

Mom walked into the kitchen with the little slimer. "I'll change her diaper." She laughed.

"Good. And if I were you, I'd hurry, because I can smell her all the way across the room."

"Elliot? . . . After I change her diaper, will you and Jonathan wheel the carriage up and down the side- walk? Maybe Ellie will take a nap."

"Do I have to?" I groaned, still trying to scrub off the slime. "Suppose someone sees me wheeling a baby carriage?"

"I want to walk her, Grammie," Jonathan said.

"Only if Elliot goes with you. You can't do it by yourself."

I groaned again.

"Please, Elliot? Please? I want to walk Ellie. I want to walk Ellie."

"Okay. Okay." Geez. "Get her ready," I said to my mother.

I don't know why anybody calls it baby-*sitting*. I didn't have a chance to sit down all day.

"Hey, I'm pushing it, Jonathan," I said as the two of us maneuvered the carriage from the driveway to the front sidewalk. "You're pushing too fast. She's going to get whiplash."

"What's that net thing for?" he asked, slowing down.

"It's to keep the bugs out. You don't want bugs chewing on your sister, do you?"

Jonathan shook his head and we kept walking. "Look. Her eyes are closing already," he said as we got to Mrs. Pagano's house. We turned around. "She likes us walking her, huh, Elliot?"

I'm glad somebody likes it. I just hoped nobody I knew saw me doing it . . . walking with a baby carriage. I almost didn't believe it myself. What would any of the guys say if they saw me walking a baby carriage? I was just lucky everybody was on vacation.

"Hi!"

Jonathan turned. "Look who it is, Elliot."

I could see her in the corner of my eye.

14

THE WORM TURNS

CORINNE MORRISEY.

Of all people to see me pushing a baby carriage, it would have to be her. What was she doing over on my street, anyway? It was bad enough I had to see her all the time over at Goog's. Now she was coming over to my house, too. I knew I should have had Dad put up a NO TRESPASSING sign.

I pulled Jonathan over next to me in front of the carriage as Corinne walked up the sidewalk chomping on some bubble gum. A fresh wad of bubble gum. I could smell it.

"Hi, Elliot."

"Hi."

"Finally got your cast off, huh?"

"Uh-huh."

"My arm looked weird like that, too." Her gum snapped and popped. "But mine didn't look as gross as yours, though."

"Too bad. Gross is so cool."

"Too bad you got the cast off too late to be in the play-offs and the swim championships at the pool."

"Yeah," I mumbled. "Too bad."

"Did your brother tell you I came in first in the butterfly?"

"I think he said something about it."

She was grinning. Was this girl a worm or what? Talk about obnoxious. Of course, if I wanted to, if I really, really wanted to, I could outworm her in a second. *If* I wanted to.

But . . . naaaaah.

"I still wish we could have beaten the Giants . . ." she said.

"Yeah, well . . . we . . . you gave them a good game. It was close all the way. . . ." I took a deep breath and sort of cleared my throat. "And, uh . . . you did tie it up in the seventh when you hit that double. . . . That really was a good hit. . . . Anyway, we'll beat them next year."

Corinne stopped chewing and looked at me.

"Yeah, we'll get 'em next year." Jonathan nodded in agreement. "And Corinne, you don't have to worry about Elliot taking back his old shortstop job."

"I don't?"

"Elliot can play any position. He doesn't have to just play shortstop. He's abaptable, right, Elliot?"

"Abaptable?" said Corinne.

"He means adaptable. . . . I'm very adaptable. I can play third, center field. Who knows, next year I might even pitch."

She didn't know what to say to that.

"So, Corinne, what are you doing over here? What do you want?"

"Oh, nothing. . . . I just thought I'd come over and see if you wanted to play some catch. . . ."

I watched as she peeked over Jonathan's head, trying to get a look in the carriage. "Or something."

She wanted to play catch? With me? Pul-ease.

"Well, sorry, Corinne, but as you can see—Jonathan and I are busy."

"Busy? What are y'all doing?"

"What does it look like we're doing?"

She got a dopey grin on her face. "It looks like you're pushing a baby carriage. Is there a baby in there?"

What a lamebrain. "Of course there's a baby in there. Do you think Jonathan and I would be pushing an empty baby carriage?"

Corinne leaned over the carriage. "Can I see it?"

"She's not an 'it.' She's a she, and she's sleeping. Hey, don't get so close. We don't want any germs getting all over her."

"I don't have germs," she said.

Sure. She was a germ.

Corinne peeked under the netting. "She looks sort of cute."

Sort of cute? She was real cute. What kind of eyes did Corinne Morrisey have, anyway?

"She's my sister," Jonathan piped in.

Corinne turned away from the carriage and looked at me. "Elliot, I didn't know you had a new baby sister."

Uh-oh.

"Uh . . . well . . ."

"He doesn't," said Jonathan.

Corinne stared at Jonathan. "I thought you just said she was your sister."

"I did. But she's not Elliot's sister."

"I don't get it." Corinne blew a bubble. It popped and she sucked it back into her mouth. "How can this baby be Jonathan's sister and not yours? Elliot, isn't Jonathan your brother?"

Jonathan laughed. "That's funny, huh, Elliot? She thinks you're my brother! All this time, and she thinks you're my brother!" He turned to Corinne. "He's not my brother. He's my—"

I took a deep breath. Well, I guess she was going to find out sooner or later. Here goes nothing. I said it.

"Uncle."

Corinne made one of her weird screwed-up scrunch faces. "Uncle?"

"That's right," I said. "Uncle."

"I don't believe you."

"What do you mean, you don't believe me?"

"You can't be an uncle. You're my age."

"So?"

"So, you're not an uncle."

"Am, too."

"Are not."

"Am, too," I shouted.

Jonathan tugged my T-shirt. "Is this 'word war,' Elliot?"

"No, this isn't word war," I said. (Like I would even waste my breath on word war with this Corinne Morrisey person.) "And I *am* Jonathan's uncle. Right, Jonathan?"

"Right, Elliot," he said, shaking his head.

"Then how come he doesn't call you Uncle Elliot? I've never heard him call you uncle even once."

This girl was getting on my nerves. "Because he just doesn't, that's all."

"Yeah, that's all," said Jonathan.

"Hmm," she said, staring at me, "Well, I've never met anyone my age who was an uncle."

"Well, I've been an uncle since I was four," I said in my best "so there" voice. I nodded toward the carriage. "I'm an uncle to her, too. . . . Not even just an uncle. A godfather."

"A godfather?"

"And she's even named after me."

"Really?"

"Yup," said Jonathan. "Her name is Elyse, but we call her little Ellie. And Elliot baby-sits us, too," Jonathan volunteered.

"Baby-sits? Elliot, you baby-sit?"

I wasn't sure if I should admit to that one. But Corinne didn't say it like she thought it was a dumb thing to do. She said it like she thought it was something pretty cool. In fact, I was beginning to see by the look on her wormy little face that she thought it was very cool. . . . *And* my toe was not sending out any warning tingles.

"Of course I baby-sit," I said.

"You do? You really do?"

"Well, don't you? Corinne, don't tell me you've never even baby-sat before! Not even once?"

Her gum fell out of her mouth and dropped to the sidewalk. Ha! She shook her head and peeked into the carriage again. "Uh . . . uh . . . well, my mother says I can't baby-sit for a real live baby until I'm at least thirteen."

"Gee, I baby-sit all the time."

Corinne looked back up at me. "Even her?"

"Naturally." (Jeffrey says that.) "And I hold her all

the time, too. And feed her. I just gave her a bottle."

"You did?"

"Yes, he did," Jonathan said. "Don't get too close to him. My sister just spit up all over his shirt so he still sort of stinks."

I shrugged. "It happens. She's only a baby, you know. . . . Sometimes babies throw up just for the heck of it. They can't help themselves."

Corinne nodded like she knew what I was talking about. She didn't fool me. She didn't have a clue what baby barf was all about. Not one clue.

"Yup. It's a big responsibility being an uncle. A real big responsibility."

All Corinne could say was "Wow."

"Uh, would you mind moving out of the way, Corinne? Jonathan and I are taking little Ellie for a walk. That's part of baby-sitting, too." I started to push the carriage. "Excuse us?"

"Oh . . . oh . . . sure . . ." She stepped off the sidewalk. "You are an uncle. A real uncle."

"That's right," I said. "I guess you don't have any nieces or nephews then, do you?" Corinne shook her head.

"That's what I thought."

"Um . . . Elliot?"

"Yes, Corinne?" I said as Jonathan and I pushed the carriage.

"Do you think, maybe . . . well, do you think maybe I could help y'all baby-sit?"

"Hmmm . . . well . . ."

"Please? Oh, please."

"I don't know. . . ."

"I just know I could do a good job if you show me what to do. Could you show me?"

"What do you think, Jonathan?"

"Hmmm . . . maybe. I guess you could teach her, Elliot. You know, show her the ropes."

I smiled at Jonathan. "Show her the ropes. Exactly, Jonathan."

"Would you, Elliot? And do you think one day I could hold her, too?" Corinne asked.

"Gee, I'm not sure," I said. "If we let you, you'll have to wash your hands."

"That's right," Jonathan said. "You have to wash them real good."

"Oh, I'll wash my hands," Corinne said. "Can I

help you push the carriage right now?"

"Should we let her help, Jonathan?"

He gave her the once-over. "I guess you could do it. But you have to be gentle."

"I'll be gentle. I'll be very gentle. I promise." She wiggled in between me and Jonathan and took hold of the handle.

"Like this, Elliot? Am I doing it right?"

"You're doing okay . . . for a beginner."

"And no pushing fast, right . . . *Uncle* Elliot?"

"Right, Jonathan."

"An uncle," Corinne said again as she pushed the carriage. "How about that? A real uncle. Wow."

I leaned back and tugged on Jonathan's shirt. We smiled at one another, and I slapped him a high five. Maybe there was more than one way to win the Wonder Worm Wars.

About the Author

MARGIE PALATINI grew up in a family with dozens of uncles, aunts, and cousins full of silly stories, infinite inspiration, and lots of love.

She is the author of several children's favorites, including *Piggie Pie!*, illustrated by Howard Fine, *Moosetache*, illustrated by Henry Cole, and *Elf Help*, illustrated by Mike Reed.

Margie, her husband, and their own wonderful, only-sometimes wormy nine-year-old live in New Jersey and are still a part of a big, funny, fabulous family.